# Arcadia's Gift

## An Arcadia Novel - Book 1

I0624822

## JESI LEA RYAN

*Arcadia's Gift*
An Arcadia Novel - Book 1
by Jesi Lea Ryan

ISBN 10 061571885X
ISBN 13 978-06157188-5-9

The characters and events portrayed in this book are fictitious.
Any similarity to real persons, living or dead, is coincidental and
not intended by the author.

Publisher
Jesi Lea Ryan

Cover by Phatpuppy Art
"Romance Fatal Serif" font (c) Juan Casco
Formatting: Champagne Formats

"Our bodies have five senses: touch, smell, taste, sight, hearing. But not to be overlooked are the senses of our souls: intuition, peace, foresight, trust, empathy. The differences between people lie in their use of these senses; most people don't know anything about the inner senses while a few people rely on them just as they rely on their physical senses, and in fact probably even more."

— C. JoyBell C.

# Prologue

IT FELT LIKE ripping ... ripping through me, ripping from me. A deafening roar reverberated all around as I lay flat on my back, drowning the shrieks and screams echoing on the river valley walls. My eyes were wide open, unblinking, but all I could see were abstract forms in shades of black, gray and red. A searing burn cut across both of my thighs as if I'd been struck by a flaming hot iron. My

1

flesh melted and bubbled, absorbing the phantom burning metal and shattering my femur bones like glass. Although I was screaming as loud as I could, the sound was distant, like someone screaming under water.

A hub of activity swirled around me, but I had the distinct feeling of being alone . . . alone in hell. I groped around on the cool soil at my sides, sparse patches of long grass and loose gravel, trying to remember where I was and what had happened to me. The pain prevented any coherent thoughts.

Voices. Panic all around me. Yet I was alone in my hell.

A flash of heat seared through my head, pounding rhythmically. Rust coated my tongue. The heat began to sink down my torso, leaking out of the stumps left under my hips. I sucked in jagged breaths as I realized that the heat was my blood, pumping through my arteries and spilling onto the cool ground.

*No! I don't want to die!* Again, the screams tore out of me. No one answered my cries.

My body grew colder. The pain faded to numbness. They say when you know that you are dying, your life flashes before your eyes. I knew I was dying, but curiously, it was my twin sister Lony's life that came to me in last minute mourning, not mine. I saw her love for me, even if we fought more than talked these days. I saw her fierce hope that our parents would reconcile their failed marriage and reunite, before nothing remained to salvage. I saw her boyfriend, Cane, and the lost promise of young love. A swell of love and pain filled my chest when I pictured Cane. It made no sense . . . I didn't even like him.

The forms in my vision began moving more slowly, becoming even darker. I struggled to reach out to them, but my arms were as heavy as iron weights. I opened my mouth to scream again, but only rust flavored foam escaped my throat and rolled down the corner of my mouth and into my hair. The skin on my face broke into a cold sweat as I steadily bled out.

It was almost over. I wanted my mom.

A shock of pain ripped through my chest as my heart raced, running out of blood.

*Thump-thump. Thump-thump.*

The faster my heart pumped, the less time I had left. My back reared up, head scraping the ground. My lungs heaved, panting. The forms in my vision swirled so dark they blended with the night. I reached out desperately with my hands, fingers not even finding a hand to hold. Breath rattled in my chest as it left my body for the final time and the whole world faded to black.

# Chapter 1

*The day before . . .*

YELLOW MORNING LIGHT seeped through the pink curtains of my bedroom, intruding on my Ian Somerhalder dream and nudging me awake. I brushed the crust out of my eyes and rolled over to check the time. Ugh! Why did I always have to wake up ten minutes before my alarm was set to go off? I dropped my head back onto the pillow and pulled the covers over my head. It was no use and I knew it. Those extra ten minutes of sleep were gone forever. The wisps of my dream faded away like smoke.

The sounds of morning in my house seeped into my warm blanket cave. My sister, Lony, was getting ready for school down the hall in our shared bathroom, her little radio tuned in to the local morning show. Every so often, she'd giggle at something the host or his sidekick said. Lony got up a half hour earlier than me every day so she could claim the shower —and eighty percent of the hot water —first.

In the kitchen below me, my mother hollered threats down the basement steps at my brother, Aaron, to coerce him into getting up for school. We only lived two blocks away from our high school, but Aaron still managed to be late at least twice a week.

Although I couldn't hear him, I knew my father must be sitting at the kitchen table drinking coffee and checking the sports section for last night's baseball scores.

Moisture tickled the insides of my eye lids, threatening to spill my grief. This would be Dad's last morning here with the family. He was moving out this weekend into one of the rental properties they owned, the one where the hallways between the apartments smelled like stale Vietnamese cooking.

I turned onto my side and hugged my down pillow to my chest. It was best to get the crying done and over with now. It wouldn't do any good to break down in front of the kids at school.

Anyone with two eyeballs in their head could see my parents hadn't been happy for a long time. They used to argue at night after we went to bed, usually about money, but a lot of times, just nit-picking at each other. We'd hear them down in the kitchen snapping and hissing, trying not to wake us. I should've known things were really bad when the arguing stopped. One or both of them must have given up the fight.

I had to get up if I was going to see my dad off to work. On a normal morning, I wouldn't have bothered, but today, it was important. I rubbed my face dry with the sleeves of my pajamas and crawled out from under the covers, turning off the alarm before it beeped. Time to boot Lony out of the bathroom. I crossed the hall and pushed open the door without knocking. My sister did her best to ignore me.

Everything about Lony's face was glittery and pink, from eye shadow to blush to lip gloss. She stood in front of the vanity methodically sectioning and flat-ironing her natural waves into a perfectly disciplined curtain that would hang down the middle of her back. Seeing her was like looking at myself in a funhouse mirror. Technically, we're identical right down to the DNA, but these days no one ever mixed us up. I'm more the "wash and wear" type.

"What's wrong with your eyes? Auditioning for *The Walking Dead*?"

I ignored her, stepping past to flip on the shower. I dropped my pajama bottoms and tugged my t-shirt over my head. Lony was the one person that I could change in front of without being self-conscious.

"Cady! Why do you have to fog up the mirror while I'm still getting ready?" Lony complained.

"Get ready in your room," I snapped back, stepping into the hot water and drawing the curtain closed. I heard her yank the electrical cord out of the wall and stomp off toward her bedroom in a huff. She came back a minute later to get her radio.

I took the fastest shower of my life, not even bothering to blow dry my hair. I threw on my clothes and hurried down the stairs. But when I got to the kitchen, the table was empty. Dad's coffee cup sat abandoned in the sink. He was already gone.

# Chapter 2

"**G**IRL, YOUR SISTER is a piece of work," Shawn declared as he slid into the bench seat across from me at the lunch table and set his tray down hard. Shawn Cole has been my friend since kindergarten, but as much as he liked me, he could never hide his aversion to my sister.

"What did she do now?" I asked, jamming a fork full of pasta salad into my mouth.

He rolled his eyes and complained, "Mr. McDonnell paired me up with Lony for our *semester long* chemistry project. We both know I get better grades than she does, but I just spent the last half hour having her dictate to me *her* ideas and how *she* insists we're gonna do things. I refuse to be bossed around for the next sixteen weeks by the Cheerleader from Hell. Any advice for me on how to handle her?"

"Yes," I replied, swallowing. "Pick your battles."

"Thanks," he muttered. Shawn set to work dissecting his cafeteria pizza until it was free of all veggie matter.

"Hi, guys," Bronwyn said cheerfully, taking her usual seat by my side. Bronwyn Perkins was my other best friend. We met in the first day of junior high when we showed up wearing identical outfits. In many ways, Bronwyn was more like me than my own twin. We're both quiet until you get to know us. We both love animals and work part-time at a local shelter. We listen to the same music, like the same books and think the same movie stars are cute. My high school career would royally suck without her.

"Shawn just found out that Lony is his partner for the chem term project," I explained.

"Oh, I'm sorry," Bronwyn replied, patting his arm. There was no love lost between her and my sister either. Lony thought Bronwyn was a nerd of the highest caliber, and Bronwyn thought Lony was a spoiled brat. Both were right to a certain extent, but that didn't mean I didn't love them both.

My gaze trailed over to where Lony and her friends sat at the center table, clearly the loudest group in the room. If a bomb fell out of the sky and took only Lony's table out, Dubuque Senior High would lose all of its varsity cheerleaders and most of the football team, leaving the marching band miraculously intact. At the moment, I could barely see my sister, because, Cane, had his muscular arms draped over her shoulders. They started dating almost a year ago, at the beginning of our sophomore year. Since then, Cane had become a regular fixture on our living room couch.

"Do you work tomorrow, Cady?" Bronwyn asked. She yanked the band out of her copper hair and began re-fixing her ponytail which had worked itself loose throughout the morning.

"Um, no. Dad's moving, remember? Thought I'd give

him a hand." I bent my head down over my plate, blinking like crazy to keep the tears back. Actually, my father said he didn't want my help. He planned to pay some guys from his construction crew overtime to load and unload boxes, but I didn't think I'd be able to keep myself from pitching in. Maybe he'd let me do the unpacking at his new place. If left to his own devices, I could picture him living out of cardboard boxes for the next year.

Shawn shot Bronwyn a warning look and responded, "We're sorry, Cady. We forgot. Are you okay? Wanna talk about it?"

"Not really," I sighed. I set my fork down, having lost my appetite. My friends stared at me with concern. I know they just wanted to be there for me, but I really needed to get through this day on my own. "I think I'm going to take off. I want to stop by the library before literature."

I stood up and carried my tray to the washing counter. As I passed by, I heard Lony's trilling soprano erupt into a fit of giggles. How could she behave so normally today? Didn't she care at all about our family falling apart? I took a deep breath. *Of course she cares about our family,* I reminded myself. *She just deals differently, that's all.*

I trudged up one flight of stairs and turned into the library, bustling with students avoiding the humiliation of where to sit in the cafeteria. The library was always busy the first couple weeks of school.

I wanted to check out some books on the Russian royal family for my European History class. I had a vague idea of doing a Romanov family tree for my class project later in the semester. I jotted down the call numbers of two promising books from the computer catalog and set off for the stacks. After locating a large volume on Nicholas II, I stood in the aisle reviewing the table of contents.

Suddenly, someone rounded the corner of the shelves and ran right in to me. I let out a little shriek and dropped the heavy volume on my foot, sending a white flash of pain up from my toes.

"Damn! I'm so sorry!" the guy said, before muttering under his breath, "I'm such an idiot . . ."

I bent down to rub my toe and retrieve the book splayed open on the floor. I wanted to be annoyed with him, but I didn't have the energy for it.

"Don't worry about it," I sighed. I carefully straightened the bent pages.

I didn't recognize him, but with over two thousand students, and this being the first week of school, there were lots of new faces roaming the halls. He wore a black button down over a white Flobots t-shirt and black, faded jeans. Over his eyes were thick brows and a disheveled patch of black hair. He carried a worn backpack covered in sewed-on patches of indie rock bands. Realizing I was staring, my face flushed.

His shoulders were slumped, but I couldn't tell if it was because I was so much shorter than him or if he just had poor posture.

"Are you okay?" he asked.

I wasn't okay, but my problems had nothing to do with my throbbing toe. "No, but I'll live," I replied dismissively. "What are you so into there that you couldn't watch where you were going?" I gestured to his hand where he had a finger stuck in a book to hold his page.

He held up *The Hitchhiker's Guide to the Galaxy* with a guilty expression. "It's stupid 'cause I've read it like five times already . . . ." His voice trailed off and he shifted his weight from foot to foot.

"Don't panic," I said.

His brows knitted together in question. "I'm not?"

I gestured to the book in his hand.

He grinned. "Oh, right! *Don't panic*." The boy was obviously pleased that I had read the book enough to quote from it, proving we were both card carrying members of the same nerd club.

His grin faded and his feet began doing the shuffling thing again. "Anyway . . . sorry to disturb you." He pivoted and began walking away.

"Wait!" I called after him.

He stopped and looked over his shoulder at me. Light purple shadows lingered beneath his eyes and his mouth was tight.

"Are you okay?" I asked. "You seem . . ."

The corner of his mouth twitched into a half grin, "No, but I'll live."

As a sucker for all creatures in need, human, animal or insect, I decided to introduce myself. "I'm Arcadia Day. You can call me Cady . . . everyone does."

"I know. You're in my literature class. And your sister, Avalon, has chemistry with me. Pretty names."

"Uh, thanks. I'm sorry, I never noticed you in lit, but don't feel bad, I'm not very observant." *Duh! Why did I say that?*

"No problem. I sit a few rows behind you. I recognized you a moment ago by the back of your head."

I couldn't help grinning. "So, considering I'm not so observant, and I obviously didn't pick it up in class, are you going to tell me your name?"

"Oh, yeah, sorry. I'm Bryan Sullivan. I'm new. We moved to Dubuque this summer from Portland . . . the one in

Oregon. Not Maine."

"Well, I guess we're both heading to lit, so if you'll wait for me to check this out, I'll walk to class with you."

A spark of enthusiasm flashed in his eyes briefly before he stifled it in an effort to remain cool. He gave a quick nod. In a school as large as ours, it could be difficult to make friends.

The first bell rang as I finished at the checkout counter. Bryan waited by the door, staring at his sneakers.

"I have to stop by my locker, but it's on the way," I said. "Do you have your stuff for class?"

Bryan nodded and patted his backpack. "They gave me a locker way up on the fourth floor, so it's easier if I carry most of my books with me."

We pushed through the busy halls. The noise of the crowd around us didn't make conversation very easy.

"So how are you fitting in?" I shouted. "Making friends?"

He shrugged. "My mom signed me up to play piano in the school jazz band. She thought it would help me to get to know some people. A few of the guys are cool, but we are in that talk-to-each-other-in-class-but-don't-associate-outside-of-school phase."

"Ah, I suppose it takes time," I replied. "So you play the piano?"

"Started with lessons when I was four years old. I prefer the guitar, but the school already had plenty of guitar players, so piano it is."

"That's so cool! I always wished I could play an instrument."

Lockers at our school are assigned by class and in alphabetical order, which means Lony's locker is right next to mine. She and Cane were leaning against the doors of both, staring googley-eyed at each other and blocking my access when I approached.

"Do you think you can go scrog somewhere else? I need to get into my locker."

Cane gave a Neanderthal-like grunt and Lony stuck her tongue out at me, but they did scoot over. Bryan waited by my side as I swapped my books out. Lony's eyes did a double take when she noticed the boy was actually with me, but Cane steered her off toward their next class before she could say anything. *Thank you, Jock Boy.*

I swung the metal door closed and spun the lock. "Ready?" I asked with a nervous smile.

"So, you and your sister . . . you're twins, right?" Bryan asked as we walked.

"Yeah."

"I almost didn't notice. You don't seem much alike."

"I know. We're actually identical, but you're right . . . we don't have a lot in common."

"Is she taller than you?"

"No. Lony just never leaves the house without wearing at least a three-inch heel. She's kind of a slave to fashion."

I looked down at my worn jeans and gray hoodie. *And I'm obviously not.*

The halls were beginning to empty out as students made their way into their classrooms.

"We also have a brother who's a senior here, Aaron. Do you have brothers or sisters?"

"No." He shook his head, "It's just me."

We stepped into class as the final bell rang. I slid into my desk, but glanced over my shoulder to see where Bryan sat. He gave me a melancholy grin as he rooted in his bag for a pen.

Ms. Crowell paced a circuit around the room while lecturing about the religious beliefs of ancient Greece. We were reading the Sophocles play *Antigone*.

I couldn't focus on Antigone and her family problems; I had enough of my own. I rested my chin on my fist and pretended to pay attention. I didn't want to dwell on my home life so my thoughts drifted to Bryan Sullivan. I tried to ignore the fact that he was sitting behind me, one row over, with me in his direct line of sight. I've always been a tad bit paranoid of being watched and knowing he was back there had me on edge. Instead, I tried to figure out why he seemed so distressed. Those shadows beneath his eyes were a clear indicator of lack of sleep. Maybe he hated living in Dubuque. I could certainly understand depression at moving to Iowa after living in a big city like Portland. Maybe he got in a fight with his parents and didn't sleep well the night before. Maybe he got in a fight with his girlfriend . . . or *maybe* he had to break up with his girlfriend because of the distance, and now his heart was shattered into a million pieces.

My day dreaming followed this line of thought. Bryan was an attractive guy. Well, okay, he was hot. He didn't have the traditional super-jock good looks that Cane had, and he didn't dress like a GQ model like Shawn, but there was definitely a magnetic quality in Bryan that made it hard to look away. If he smiled a little more and got some rest, he could easily be one of the best looking guys in school. It made total sense that a guy like him would have a girlfriend. What would she be like? I couldn't see him with a popular fashionista like my sister. Bryan had a sense of mystery about him, or maybe it was intelligence. He'd want a girl with those same qualities. An artist maybe?

Ms. Crowell's voice wrenched me out of my head suddenly by asking me something. I sat up straight and tried to recall the question. I opened my mouth to speak, but honestly, I had nothing.

When it became clear to everyone I hadn't been paying attention, Ms. Crowell scolded, "I'm not sure where you were just now, Miss Day, but I'd appreciate it if you re-joined the class."

A few snickers crackled around the room. The teacher strolled down the aisle and called on someone else. I sat up straighter and began taking notes to keep my mind on the lecture.

By the time the bell rang, I'd successfully put Bryan Sullivan out of my mind. I closed my notebook and gathered my things slowly. My last class of the day was French, located in the classroom just across the hall. I didn't need to go to my locker, so I waited for everyone else to file out before getting up to leave.

"Cady," Bryan's voice called from behind me. He stood with his backpack slung over his shoulder. "Where are you off to now?"

"French. Right across the hall. What about you?"

"Photography," he answered. Yeah, I figured him for the artsy type. I could totally picture him holed up in a dark room poring over black and white stills of decaying buildings.

We both stood there awkwardly for a moment. A couple of students for the next class entered the room and sat down. "Well, I guess we better get going then," I said.

When we stepped into the hallway, Bryan stopped me again. "Thank you. For talking to me, I mean."

I shrugged. "No problem. It must be hard going to a new school."

"Yeah . . . um . . ." His voice trailed off and he suddenly had trouble meeting my eyes.

I waited, not knowing if he just paused, or if he decided to stop talking.

"What?" I prompted.

He opened his mouth to speak again, but the bell rang. "I'm going to be late. I'll see you Monday."

Bryan jogged off down the hall and rounded the corner. *What a strange guy*, I thought.

"Mademoiselle Day?" Madame Deveraux called to me from the door of her French class. "Entrez vous?"

I nodded and ducked inside.

# Chapter 3

THE FRONT DOOR was already unlocked when I got home from cross country practice. Our first meet was still two weeks away, but I couldn't wait. I've always been more of a track sprinter than a distance runner, but I'd worked on distance training over the summer and was going to enter some longer races this year.

Cane lay sprawled out on my living room floor watching baseball highlights on ESPN. He'd kicked his sneakers off, giving me a view of the gaping hole in the toe of his sock. He didn't turn to look hearing me come in. That wasn't unusual. For some reason, he had trouble making eye contact with me. Maybe he didn't think I was cool enough for him or something.

Lony sat on the sofa with her feet on the coffee table, painting her toenails. I could hear the head-banging wails of what passed for music in Aaron's world reverberating up from the basement. So much for doing my homework in peace.

Backpack in hand, I began ascending the stairs to my room. Maybe I could see if Bronwyn wanted go to the public library for a while. With Dad moving, I should get my homework done tonight in case I didn't feel up to it later in the weekend.

"Hey, Cady!" Lony called out. "Come 'ere a sec."

I sighed and poked my head into the living room. "What?"

Lony grinned at me like a Cheshire cat. "Who was that uber-hot emo guy you were with today?"

"Bryan Sullivan. He's new." I tried to turn away, but Lony kept talking.

"He's in my chem class, but he doesn't talk much. Were you like assigned to show him around or something? He's a junior, right?"

"I assume so. We have lit together. And I wasn't giving him a tour of the school. I just walked to class with him."

"Do you like him?" Lony teased with a sing-songy tone. Cane cocked his head to listen, as if interested in my answer.

"Jeez, Lon! I talked to the guy for a total of ten minutes. Don't you have cheerleading practice or something?" I asked. Changing the subject with Lony is easy if you bring the topic around to her.

She rolled her eyes dramatically. "Cady, do you live under a rock or something? Tonight is the first football game." She gestured to Cane wearing his jersey which looked deflated without the hulking pads beneath it. All of the players wore their jerseys to school on game days. "There's no practice because we cheer tonight."

"Oh. Well . . . break a leg," I replied and hurried upstairs. I wanted to get out of there before Lony could guilt me into attending the game to watch her jump up and down in her pleated skirt, chanting loosely rhyming lines meant to pump up the crowd.

I hung my bag on the back of my desk chair. My bedroom was carefully decked out by my mother in every possible shade of pink. I hated it, but there's no arguing with her when it comes to interior decorating. Mom is a realtor, and a successful one at that. Even though we've lived in this house for ten years and have no plans to move anytime soon, my mother insists on keeping the entire house in perfect "open-house" condition at all times. The one exception being Aaron's room, but as long as he keeps his mess in the basement where she can pretend it doesn't exist, she leaves him alone about it.

I never liked the color pink, but somehow as infants it was determined that my color would be pink and Lony's would be purple. That's how people kept us straight, I guess. Anyway, the result is that almost every Christmas or birthday gift we have ever received from our extended family had been identical, but in either pink or purple. Like if our Grandma Nora were to get us sweaters, Lony's would be a soft lavender and mine would be some hideous shade of Pepto-Bismol.

I pressed the power button on my computer, and it purred to life. While it booted up, I called Bronwyn.

"Hey, I'm going to do the loser thing and spend my Friday night at the library. Wanna come?"

"Just a sec, I have to go to my office," she said. I heard her walk the phone into her pantry and shut the door. She had a little stool in there where she could talk in semi-privacy. Her parents didn't believe children should be allowed phones in their bedrooms.

"The library actually sounds like more fun than what

I have planned," she said softly. "My parents are making me go to a lock-in at the church." Bronwyn's father was the minister the New Life Bible Church, and her mother served as the church secretary.

"Aren't lock-ins for like middle school kids?"

"Yeah. It's going to be me and a bunch of sixth graders. Mother says I have to go to set a good example." Her mocking tone was the extent of her rebelliousness.

While they'd always been very hospitable toward me, the Perkins' tended to hold Bronwyn's reins pretty tightly. She wasn't allowed much of a social life outside of school and church functions. They wouldn't even let her stay overnight at my house because I have a brother under the same roof. Apparently, Pastor Tom thinks Aaron is some sort of teenage Casanova with designs on seducing my friends while they sleep.

"Maybe we can do something Sunday after church?" she suggested.

"I probably shouldn't plan anything. I don't know how I'll feel with my dad leaving and all."

"Sorry for my comment at lunch."

"Don't worry about it. I'm just really on edge about the whole separation thing right now. God, my eyes are tearing up just thinking about it!" I rubbed my face with the hood of my sweatshirt. I sniffed loudly into the phone. "Sorry . . ."

"I know. How are Lony and Aaron taking it?"

"Well, you know how Aaron is. I tried to talk to him a couple of days ago, and he just shrugged and returned to his underground lair."

"I don't know why boys always think they have to be so stoic."

"I know, right? And Lony . . . she's convinced that our

parents are going to get back together and refuses to take any of it seriously."

"Do you think they will . . . get back together?"

"I don't know. Doubt it. With both of them running their own businesses, they never see each other. I have a feeling this 'trial separation' is really the first step in the divorce."

"Unfortunately, it usually is. Darn! I just heard the garage door, so Father's home. I better run. If you need to talk this weekend, give me a call."

"I will."

After we hung up, I took a few minutes to check my email and my Facebook account. I find it hilarious that Lony has 847 friends on her Facebook, and I have thirty-two. Well, at least I actually know and talk to all of mine. I answered a few messages and poked around online a bit, but when I heard my mother come home, I logged off.

"You don't need to order pizza," my mother was saying to Aaron when I entered the kitchen. "There's leftover casserole in the fridge. Heat that up."

Aaron shuffled out of the room in his stocking feet, muttering under his breath. Mom had kicked off her pumps and stood on one leg, massaging the ball of her foot.

"Hi, Mom," I said, walking to the fridge to get a Diet Pepsi. "Busy day?"

"Oh, aren't they all? I just stopped to get the car-charger for my Blackberry. I have two houses to show in Asbury, and then I'm going straight to the football game to see Lony cheer. Do you have plans tonight?"

Mom slipped her shoes back on and opened the junk drawer. She extracted a tangle of chargers for various electronics and began to un-weave the one she needed from the mass.

"No plans. Just homework."

She leveled her gazed on me. "Cady, you do realize you are the only teen in the Tri-State area who voluntarily does homework on a Friday night, right?"

"I have to get it done tonight, so I can help Dad move tomorrow."

"Oh, no you're not! Your father and I talked about it, and we don't want you kids in the middle of this. We want you all to go find stuff to do with your friends tomorrow and stay away from here. He has enough people to help him."

"But, Mom," I reasoned, standing with my hand on my hip, "We're already in the middle of this. I can't let Dad do this alone."

Mom let out an audible sigh and rubbed her temple. "Arcadia Marie, don't argue with me. Think of your dad. This is going to be hard enough on him, he doesn't need an audience."

I gritted my teeth to keep from talking back. There was no use in arguing with her when she made her mind up about something. I poured my soda into a glass of ice.

"Maybe you and Lony should go shopping tomorrow," she suggested. "It'll be good for you to spend some time together."

The last thing I wanted to do was spend the day at the mall with Lony, but just then Lony flitted into the kitchen, so again, I held my tongue.

"Hey, Mamasita!" Lony said, giving our mother a peck on the cheek. "Still coming to the game tonight?"

"Of course, hun, but I'll have to meet you there. Got an appointment right now. See you later!"

Mom waved good-bye and ran out the door with her charger in hand.

"Are you coming to the game tonight?" Lony asked, grabbing two sodas out of the fridge.

"I didn't plan on it. I have some homework to do," I answered, sipping on my drink.

"Only you would do homework on a Friday night," Lony complained, stalking back to the living room.

I went to my bedroom and spread my textbooks across the bed. I took studying very seriously, but then, I had to. I wasn't one of those naturally gifted people who absorb knowledge without trying. I make good grades, but I need to work very hard to do it. College was still two years away, but I really wanted to get accepted to a school out of state. I had been thinking about someplace in New England, but recently, California sounded good, too. Really, I just wanted to get out of Iowa. Dubuque's not so bad, but I didn't want to spend my whole life here, either. I reached for my French book and set to work.

The sky turned a bruised purple outside my window. I'd finished my French and history and was working on trigonometry when my dad poked his head in my bedroom door.

"Hey, Bug," he greeted. His work clothes were a bit dusty from hanging around job sites all day, and his eyes looked tired. My dad is a general contractor who builds homes and small commercial buildings. He'd been sleeping in the guest room ever since the big announcement was made. Not the most comfortable bed in the house.

"Hi, Dad. What's up?" I asked, trying to act casual, but not quite succeeding with the knot in my throat.

"Just got home and it looks like everyone is gone except you and me."

"Yeah, Lony is cheering at the game tonight. Mom went to see her. I don't know where Aaron ran off to. I heard his truck leave about an hour ago."

My dad leaned against the door frame. He was still a handsome man, even if his waist was a little thicker and his hair a little thinner. His almond-colored eyes were exactly like mine.

"It's Friday night. Are you just going to do homework?" he asked.

"I don't know," I shrugged, closing my book. "Do you have something else in mind?"

"How would you like to go to a movie with your old man? We can see anything you want as long as it's not a tear-jerker."

"I'd love to." I'd always been a daddy's girl.

# Chapter 4

MY MOTHER GOT her way, and Saturday morning found me packed into the car with Lony and on our way to the mall. The official orders from both of our parents were to stay gone all day, but Dad said I could stop by his new place Sunday afternoon to help him settle in.

It's not like I hated my sister or anything . . . we just had nothing to talk about. It's not like when we were little and inseparable. Then, she'd been my best friend, more than that even. We finished each other's sentences and spoke in a secret language all our own. When our parents finally moved us into separate bedrooms at seven years old, it was six months before I stopped sneaking into Lony's bed after our parents went to sleep.

High school ruined everything. The summer before freshman year, puberty struck with a vengeance. We each gained five inches of height and added the perfect curves to compliment our slender frames. Lony loved her new body.

She relished in the attention it brought her from boys at the public swimming pool. She would parade back and forth in front of the concession stand in her striped bikini, giving coy glances to the boys as she passed. I was slower to accept the changes. I'd always been more athletic than Lony, competing in cross country and track at school and gymnastics on the weekends at a local club. But the growth spurt had knocked me off my rhythm. That summer I spent almost every day at the YMCA reacquainting myself with my body and its limits. While I was too bulky to stay competitive in gymnastics, I was running sprints like Hermes. By the time school started, I was in great physical condition, ready to compete for a shot on the Varsity track team. Lony was ready to compete in a whole different way . . . she wanted the title of Most Popular Girl in School, and was willing to step on anyone to get it.

Since we had an entire Saturday to kill and the Dubuque mall was pathetically inadequate, Lony crossed the bridge spanning the Mississippi River into Wisconsin, heading toward Madison. Three hours later, I sat outside a dressing room reading a comic book on my e-reader while my sister modeled a seemingly endless series of homecoming dresses for me.

"You really should go to the dance. I mean, it's Homecoming. Isn't that like a right of passage or something?" She'd been badgering me the entire ride up to Madison about my lack of interest in school activities.

"You don't give yourself enough credit," she rattled on. "I know like five guys who would take you if you wanted to go. If you were desperate, you could even ask Shawn. Not very romantic, but at least he can dance. What do you think of this one?"

My sister stood before me in a rose-tinted halter dress with a dangerously low neckline.

"I think you'd never get out of the house in it," I muttered.

Her face fell into a pout. "You're right. Too bad, though. I look hot."

Lony slipped back into the dressing room to wriggle into something else. A moment later she was back out in a silvery-blue number, twirling in the three-way mirror.

"What about that emo guy?" she asked.

"Huh?"

"You know . . . that guy you were walking with yesterday . . . Byron?"

"Bryan," I sighed. "What about him?"

Lony planted her fists on her hips and gave me an exasperated look. "Aren't you paying attention? You should ask him to Homecoming! I bet he looks good dressed up. Just don't let him wear all black, it's depressing."

"No, Lon," I said, slipping my e-reader back in my bag. "I don't want to go. I dance like an idiot, I hate the music they play, and there are no boys in school that I'm even remotely interested in." My stomach ached with hunger, so I decided to move Lony along. "Maybe we should hit the food court. I'm starving."

"Fine," she replied, even though clearly she was not. She gave the dress one last twirl. "But what do you think about this one?"

"I don't know. It's kind of plain. I like it, but it's not really your style."

"Yeah. You're right. Well, give me a sec to change and we'll go."

We were sitting in the bustling food court, surrounded

by a circle of fast food places, when Lony started in again on my boring social life.

"Why don't you come out with me tonight?" Lony asked, dipping her French fry in mayonnaise before eating it. "A bunch of us are going out to the Mines of Spain. You should come. We never hang out anymore."

"That's because we don't have anything in common. It's not personal; it's just the way it is."

"No, you just have a thing against my friends. I don't know why, they like you well enough."

"Well, you don't like to do stuff with my friends, either." I argued, shoving a forkful of salad in my mouth.

"Not true! I went to the movies with you and Shawn just two weeks ago."

"Yeah, but Cane came with, and you made out with him the whole time. Do you even remember what movie we saw?"

"So that's it?" she asked, dramatically tossing her fry back onto her tray. "Are you jealous that I have a boyfriend and you don't?"

"Oh, please," I muttered. I set my fork down. "How can you even ask that? Of course I'm not jealous of Cane. Maybe the reason I don't like to hang out with you is because you're constantly lecturing me. Back off!"

I stood up from the table, dumped my garbage in the trash can and waited for Lony on a bench by the mall exit. If I'd had the keys to the car, I would've been tempted to leave without her. Lony followed a few minutes later, with a look of apology on her face.

"I'm sorry, Cady," she said. When I didn't answer, she sat down on the bench next to me and continued. "I was being bossy again, wasn't I? I don't mean to be that way, but you're my little sister."

I kicked my shoe at a scuff mark on the tiled floor. "Eight minutes does not make me your *little* sister," I said for the thousandth time in my life. The familiar joke cut the tension between us somewhat, and I broke into a reluctant smile.

Lony put her arm around me in a half-hug. "I just miss you, that's all. We used to be best friends, and now I hardly see you. It shouldn't matter that we have different friends and like different things. We're twins, not clones."

"I know. I miss you, too," I replied honestly.

"So does that mean you're gonna go out with me tonight? I promise if you're miserable, we can go home."

Being miserable was virtually guaranteed, but I'm not one to fight a losing battle. "Fine . . ."

With a triumphant grin, Lony pulled me off the bench and drove us home.

# Chapter 5

AMY SUTHERLAND, A friend of my sister's, was in the middle of telling me a rather boring and overly-detailed story about a guy she met during the summer while working at a resort in the Wisconsin Dells. I pretended to be interested and wondered how much time I'd have to sit there before it was socially appropriate to ask Lony to take me home. We were hanging out on the hood of Amy's Chevy in a small parking area at the Mines of Spain. At one point in time, the river bluffs along the Mississippi were full of lead, attracting miners to the area. After the minerals in the hills were exhausted, the state sectioned off the area as a nature preserve filled with hiking trails winding through the forest. Kids weren't supposed to loiter there after dark, but that just added to the appeal.

Amy didn't need much encouragement to keep her chatter flowing. I nodded once in a while and made noises where appropriate. Something about her story made me doubt the existence of this summer dream boy. Honestly, I couldn't imagine any guy finding her interesting enough to waste a whole summer on. My shoe rhythmically kicked her car tire to the beat of a song in my head.

Twenty or thirty other kids from school were with us. If the DNR were to spot us while on patrol, they'd assume we were up to no good and kick us out. In reality, we were just a bunch of kids standing around and talking with nothing better to do on a Saturday night. I could see Lony leaning against Cane's truck, pretending to thumb through his iPod for some music, but the glare fixed on her face along with her repeated glances in Cane's direction told a different story. He stood talking with a petite redhead who came with some kids from Hempstead High. While I didn't notice any outright flirting going on, I knew Lony must be jealous. Cane was easily the handsomest guy in our school. He had sun-streaked blond hair and soft green eyes. As he laughed a big throaty chuckle at something the girl said, I noticed his smile looked like something straight out of a toothpaste commercial. I could understand what some girls saw in him, even if he wasn't my type.

"Hey," Matt Kutch called out, "Anyone want to go for a walk?"

"Not on the cliffs!" Lony replied. "I'll go if we stay in the low areas."

Everyone in Dubuque knew how dangerous the Mines of Spain could be at night. Every few years, some teenager would accidentally fall off one of the cliffs or drown in the Mississippi River which rolled on the edge of the park. Usually, those incidents involved alcohol, which was thankfully absent tonight, but even a sober person could misjudge the footing on the narrow trails and tumble down the rocks.

"Wanna walk?" Amy asked me. I glanced around and it

seemed only Matt, Lony and Cane were planning to go. I had no intention of letting my sister leave me here with a bunch of kids I hardly knew.

"Okay," I shrugged, sliding off the hood of the car.

Amy and I followed Matt onto the dark trail surrounded by tall trees in full foliage. He had a large flashlight from his glove box that he used to illuminate the trail and keep us from stumbling too much. Cane also had a small flashlight, but it wasn't long before he and Lony started to lag behind. I peeked back every few minutes to make sure I could still see their beam following in the distance.

"I'm surprised you came out tonight, Cady," Matt commented. "I never see you outside of school." I really didn't know Matt all that well, and if it weren't for being Lony's sister, he probably wouldn't even know my name. My impression of the tall, gangly boy was formed in the one class we'd had together our freshman year. Matt tried to hide is complete inability to do algebra by goofing off, driving our teacher insane. Truthfully, I thought he could be obnoxious when he had an audience around to encourage him, but he didn't seem too bad when he let his guard down and acted like himself.

"Well, Lony kind of made me," I answered, picking a leaf off of a low-hanging limb and twirling it between my palms.

Matt and I made awkward conversation while Amy tagged at our heels, complaining about the mosquitoes.

We had been hiking for a while when I started to hear raised voices behind us. Lony and Cane were arguing, but I couldn't make out the words.

"Jeez, all they do is fight," Amy muttered.

Amy was right. Lony and Cane preferred bickering as

32

their main form of communication. My entire family was getting sick of listening to it. Lony had a quick temper, and clueless Cane couldn't stop himself from setting her off. Most of their arguments revolved around something he said or didn't say, did or didn't do, that Lony took personally. I suspected her issue tonight revolved around the cute redhead he'd been talking to back in the parking lot. Maybe that's why I didn't feel the need to run out and get a boyfriend. It looked like too much aggravation.

The trail opened up into a clearing as it drew closer to the Mississippi. Railroad tracks snaked their way along the edges of the river on both sides. Dubuque actually sits at the corner of three states: Iowa on the west side of the river, Wisconsin and Illinois on the east. Across the mile-wide river, the Illinois bluffs were dark and peaceful under the bright moonlight.

Matt led us over to a couple of boulders to wait for Lony and Cane to catch up. Amy started in on a story about a recent concert she attended where she snuck backstage to meet the band, and the drummer taught her to do a drum roll. From the expression on his face, Matt wasn't buying it any more than I was. I kept my ear out for my sister. I could see her and Cane about fifty yards away walking along the tracks toward us. I still couldn't hear what the argument was about, but the whiney tone in Lon's voice echoed off the valley walls and I thought she might be crying.

Beyond Amy's talking, I detected what sounded like the rumble of a boat motor in the distance. My eyes scanned the water, but I didn't see anything. I couldn't imagine why a boat would be on the river in the dark. The Mississippi was notoriously dangerous. The rumble got louder, closer . . . surely I'd be able to spot a boat that big even in the darkness. I couldn't tell where it was coming from. Sound travels oddly, almost deceptively, on the river valley. Sound waves bounce off the limestone cliffs and roll over the water strangely. When the rumble turned into a roar, Matt and I looked at each other with wide-eyes.

In the end, it was the spotlight blazing down the track, not the roar of the engine which alerted me to the train rounding the limestone curve of the cliff at the river's edge, less than two hundred yards from my sister.

What happened next took only seconds. I jumped to my feet and screamed Lony's name. In the glare of the single headlight, both faces stood frozen like deer. Matt and I ran over the rocky ground toward them as fast as our legs could move. Cane snapped to attention first and ran off the tracks. When he noticed Lony wasn't following, he turned back yelling her name and reaching out for her arm. Lony snapped out of her shock and tried to run, but the heel of her sandal caught the edge of the wood rail, sending her sprawling to the ground. In the same instant, a power surge flashed through my body, twenty yards away, flinging me onto my back. The world faded to black.

# Chapter 6

MY HEARING CAME back first. An annoying rhythmic beep plucked on my nerves like harp strings. I thought it was my alarm clock, and I was late for school. I tried to shut it off, but my arm felt as if it were pinned at my side by a tangle of snakes.

I cracked my eyes open to see a strange room with dingy, white wallpaper and a TV mounted from the ceiling. *Where am I?* I struggled to call out, my vocal cords burned and something was jammed in my mouth. Although I could breathe fine, the fat tube down my throat sent me into a claustrophobic panic. My hands fumbled like they were wearing thick mittens, but I managed to rip the IV tube out of my arm. The annoying beeps escalated, sending a nurse dashing into the room to stop me just as I began wrestling with the tube in my mouth.

"Relax, Honey," the nurse murmured as she pinned my arms to my sides. "Be still. You're going to hurt yourself."

My arm leaked crimson dots onto the crisp sheet from

the IV hole. I tried slowing my breathing down to suppress the panic urges. The nurse brushed a sweaty lock of hair back from my face and checked me over carefully. She smelled like vanilla and hand sanitizer. A plastic nametag on her shirt told me her name was Jenny.

"It's okay . . . you're going to be okay. Just relax," Jenny whispered as she pressed a call button for the nurse's station and asked for a doctor to be paged. My eyes watered with fear, and I bit down on the tube tightly. She swiftly cleaned up my bloody arm and re-inserted the fat IV needle. A doctor in a navy blue scrubs hurried in and began asking the nurse all kinds of questions. Their voices seemed too loud, and I closed my eyes to fend off a headache.

"Open your eyes if you can hear me?" a deep voice asked.

I opened my eyes again to see the doctor leaning over me. He had shadowy stubble on his face, and his breath smelled like stale coffee.

"My name is Dr. Gibler. I'm going to ask you a few questions so I can examine you," the doctor explained. "There's a tube in your mouth which is helping you breathe. As long as the tube is in, you will not be able to speak. I'll get it out in a moment. Until then, you can answer my questions with blinking your eyes, okay? One blink for 'yes,' two blinks for 'no.' Do you understand me?"

I tried to nod, but my throat burned with the motion. Now, I understood the blinking thing. I blinked once to let the doctor know I understood him.

He crossed to a sink along the wall and washed his hands.

"Do you know where you are?" he asked.

Duh, a hospital. One blink.

He dried his hands on a paper towel. "Do you remember what happened? Why you are here?"

I tried to remember, but I couldn't focus my hazy thoughts. Two blinks.

"Okay. I'm going to remove you from the ventilator. This may be uncomfortable and your throat will ache for a while. On the count of three, I want you to take a deep breath and blow it out through your mouth. Are you ready?"

One blink.

Dr. Gibler deflated the cuff and counted to three. When I blew out, he pulled the plastic tube from my throat in one swift motion. Even though the flesh inside felt enflamed, I sputtered and coughed. Nurse Jenny handed me a Dixie cup of ice chips and popped a couple into my mouth. The cold liquid felt blissfully refreshing on my dry, gluey tongue. While she took my vitals and noted them in my chart, the doctor began asking me questions.

"Do you know where you are?"

"H-H-Hospital?" My voice came out all hoarse and shaky.

"Good. Can you tell me your name?"

"Arcadia Marie Day. Cady."

"Very good, Cady. Now, can you tell me what year this is?"

"2012. How long have I been here?" I asked, tilting the cup to my lips for more ice chips. I knew he was just checking my mental status, but his questions annoyed me.

"Three and a half days," Dr. Gibler answered. "You were admitted on Saturday night and it is now shortly before noon on Wednesday."

"Wow . . . ." It was strange and confusing to think that I had lost three days of my life.

"Are you in any pain?" Dr. Gibler asked.

I ran through my body parts mentally. "Um . . . headache. Not bad though. I think it's just from that constant beeping."

The doctor's brow wrinkled in confusion before he recalled the heart monitor. He reached up and flipped the volume off.

I tried a weak smile, "Thanks."

"Cady, do you remember what happened before you lost consciousness?"

I concentrated hard. I remembered having a vivid nightmare about getting run over by a train, but I couldn't remember being in any kind of accident.

"Tell me what you're thinking," Dr. Gibler inquired. "What do you remember?"

"A dream. I remember having a dream. It was weird."

"Tell me about it."

"It was so real! I got hit by a train. Only it wasn't me really. I was my sister . . . or maybe I was inside my sister's body. I could feel every pain and sensation as if it were really happening to me. I could taste the blood in my mouth . . . Seriously, I've never felt so much pain in my life. I didn't know dreams could do that."

An odd expression clouded over Dr. Gibler's face, a mixture of confusion and sorrow. "You felt it? Like physically?"

I pressed my eyes closed and tried to block out the horrifying images from my dream. "Yes, I felt it. I felt legs being severed by the wheels of a train. I felt my temperature drop as my blood drained from my body." I shook my head to clear away the images. My belly roiled with nausea. "I can remember every detail of the dream, but I can't remember the accident that landed me in here."

"Accident?" the doctor asked, casting a glance at Jenny. "Cady, you weren't in an accident. In fact, there's not a scratch on you." He turned to the nurse. "Page her parents, please."

Jenny draped her stethoscope around her neck and stepped out of the room.

"What's happened?" I asked. "Am I dying?"

"No, you're going to be fine." The doctor fiddled with my chart, staring at it, but not really reading it. Stalling.

"Tell me. What happened?" I pleaded.

"Let's wait for your parents. Your father is just down in the cafeteria."

"No," I insisted. "Tell me now!" I attempted to sit up, but my head spun and I slumped back down.

"Okay, Cady," he said as he pulled a chair alongside the bed and leaned with his forearms balanced on the metal guardrail. "I have some rather disturbing news." He took a deep breath before continuing. "It's your sister, Avalon. She was in an accident. She was struck by a train and killed Saturday night. I'm so sorry."

The doctor paused to gauge my reaction. My face remained frozen, but my mind wheeled about in a dozen different directions.

"What you remember was not a dream. In fact, you've been in a coma, which means you were so deeply unconscious that your brain did not go through the normal sleep cycles. You couldn't have had any dreams."

Spontaneous tears welled in my eyes, but I blinked them away. He must be wrong. Lony can't be gone. I wanted to argue with him, to tell him he must be wrong. "W-w-w . . . ?" I sputtered.

"Your father is downstairs in the cafeteria. Nurse Jenny just went to get him, and she'll phone your mother. Your parents have been taking turns staying at the hospital with you."

"But . . . what about me?" I asked, still confused. "What happened to me? Why am I . . . you know . . . here?"

The doctor pursed his lips as if in deep thought. "Honestly, we're not quite sure what happened to you. We were hoping you could fill us in. When you were first brought to the ER, we assumed you had been hit also, but there were no injuries. Then, we figured you passed out from the emotional shock of it all, but then your blood pressure dropped dangerously low and your breathing became irregular. It was clear that this was no ordinary swoon."

It was all too much to process. To say that my heart was breaking over the loss of my twin was an understatement. My hands trembled with emotion that needed to escape but had nowhere to go. Ordinary tears were not enough of an outlet. Suddenly, I felt naked and adrift in the clouds. I never realized how tightly my life was bound to my sister's until the comfortable weight of her was gone.

The doctor took a few minutes to examine me and make notes in my chart, but everything he did and said turned into a blur. Flashes of the dream —or were they memories? — roamed about in my head. The more I tried to hold them down, the more real they became. I squeezed my eyes shut.

"Oh, thank God!" my dad cried as he ran through the doorway and fell on me with a tight embrace. Once my face was safely buried in the crook of his shoulder, I breathed in the comforting familiar scent and let the tears loose.

Dad rocked me in his arms and pressed his lips to the part of my hair. When he finally drew back to look at my face, he appeared ten years older. Huge gray bags hung below his eyes and his skin looked chalky. "The nurse called your mother. She'll be here in a few minutes. Doc, do you know what happened to her yet? Will she be all right?"

Dr. Gibler nodded and gestured for my father to take a seat in the chair beside my bed. My father covered his hand in mine, holding on a little too tightly. One, or maybe both of us, was shaking.

The doctor's kind eyes were surrounded by deep wrinkles. "I'm so sorry, Cady . . . about all of this. I can't explain why you were overcome the way you were. Shock is still an area of the human mind that doctors are unclear on." He went on to explain that there are two kinds of shock, emotional and physical, and they are the mind's way of protecting a person from trauma. What I had experienced was an emotional shock, but for some reason, my body had responded to it as if I had been the one physically traumatized. "I've consulted with a shock expert at the University of Iowa and he has never seen a case of emotional trauma setting off physical symptoms to this extent. The erratic breathing and heart-rate, the drop in blood pressure, the coma. The only thing we can assume is that it was the extreme circumstances of witnessing the accident which caused it."

My father's face crumpled, and I knew he was thinking about Lony. So was I. She couldn't be gone. Lony was so beautiful and fun and young—she loved life! And what about me? What is a twin without the other?

I didn't have time to ponder it further. My mother burst in the door all tears and loudness. She seemed both overjoyed at my consciousness and deeply scarred from the death of her other daughter. She nudged my father out of the way so she could hug me and sob onto my hospital gown. There was a thick wall of tension between my parents. It was nothing that I could see really, more of an intuition. Something more was going on with them.

"Doctor," my father asked, "How soon can we take her home?" Mom raised her head for the answer. For the first time in years, she had left the house without her face made up.

Dr. Gibler replied, "Well, Cady's vitals are strong. Her heart rate and blood pressure are back to normal. I suspect the worst is behind her now, but I'd like to keep her overnight for monitoring. We still don't know what caused her to lose consciousness for so long."

My father nodded, but my mother's lips formed a hard line. "Don't you think she'll be more comfortable in her own bed? It's really inconvenient having her away from home, and she looks fine."

Something else was off about my mom, other than her lack of cosmetics. Her gestures were a little too broad, her words slightly slurred. Dad must have noticed it too, because his eyes narrowed in on her face.

"Besides," she continued waving her hands around, "We have a funeral to prepare for."

Both my father and I flinched at the word funeral. All of a sudden, I felt the anguish my parents were going through with one daughter in the hospital and one in the morgue. My stomach rolled again. I started to gag and the doctor shoved a plastic pan in front of me. Nothing came out, but the heaves strained the muscles of my abdomen.

"Julia!" my father snapped, darting his eyes toward me. "Not here."

My mother set her shoulders back and she stomped out of the room, shoving the door hard. My father gave me an apologetic look before following her out into the hall.

"It's going to be fine, Cady," the doctor assured me. "As you must know, they're under a lot of stress. This isn't easy on anyone. Can I get you anything?"

I shook my head. I just wanted to be alone.

# Chapter 7

THE TIME BETWEEN waking from my coma and the funeral was a complete daze. I'd been released from the hospital on Thursday morning only to stay in my bed until I had to get up for my sister's wake Saturday morning. Bronwyn came over, at my grandmother's request, to help get me ready. After a couple of lame attempts at conversation, she gave up and went about the motions of getting me ready in silence. I sat on the toilet lid in my robe while she brushed and dried my hair with a feather-light touch. We both knew if she tugged too hard I might shatter.

I put on the dress that someone set out for me without really looking at it, thankful that I didn't have to make any decisions for myself. Mom left for the funeral home early with Grandma Nora, so Bronwyn drove my brother and me over in her mother's minivan. Aaron was dressed in one of our dad's suits and kept fingering the knot of his tie, trying to loosen it enough for comfort, but not so much that our mother would freak out on him.

I'd been in Grandview Funeral Home a few years earlier, when my Grandpa Bill passed away, so I thought I knew what to expect. I learned really quickly that an elderly man's funeral, even one who was respected and loved like my Grandpa, couldn't compare with that of a popular sixteen-year-old cheerleader. Parked cars lined the avenue on both sides of the street for three blocks. It seemed as if everyone in Dubuque was here.

"I better drop you guys off at the door," Bronwyn said. "It's gonna take me forever to find a parking place, and I don't want you to be late." She turned into the lot and pulled up in the fire lane to let us out.

"Thanks," Aaron muttered before hopping out of the back.

My posterior felt glued to the passenger seat.

Aaron didn't notice I wasn't behind him until he turned to hold the funeral home door open for me. His already grim face fell a little further, and he returned to retrieve me from the vehicle.

"Come on, Cady," he said, opening the passenger door and unhooking my seatbelt for me. "It sucks, but we have to do this. If it's too awful, I'll find a way to take you home early, okay?"

"Okay," I replied, my voice dry and crackled. With a hand on his shoulder to steady myself, I slid out of the seat. Leaning on my brother seemed to magnify my sorrow, and I struggled with the heaviness in my chest. It was just the two of us now. The odd feeling vanished as Aaron, seeing that I was steady on my feet, started walking ahead of me toward the building. I flashed a weak wave to Bronwyn as she pulled away from the curb.

Several people, mostly students from school, stared at

us as we made our way inside the building. The pity in their eyes felt strong enough to touch, making me long for the safety of my bed.

Aaron took a deep breath and let it out with a whoosh. "All right, let's get this over with."

Aunt Tina, our dad's younger sister who drove in from Chicago, met us right inside the door.

"There you are!" she exclaimed, drawing us both into a tight hug, her bleach blond extensions tickling my nose. "The family seating is in the reserved rows up front. They just started the receiving line."

Aunt Tina crushed my hand in hers and dragged me through the crowd. Aaron followed behind us. My emotions were all over the map, making me feel like a computer getting ready to short circuit. I'd taken half of a Valium before leaving the house. Not enough to make me sleepy, but just enough to separate my mind from my body with a thick layer of numbness. I could sense tension and sorrow vibrating through me, but at the same time, it was like it was happening to someone else. Even with the medication, the pressure of the crowd triggered claustrophobia, making my chest heave and my palms dampen. Between that and the mass of people making the air thick and stuffy, my stomach tumbled with nausea.

I was halfway up the aisle before I spotted the white wooden casket, the door hinged open to show the lavender-tinted satin interior. I snapped my gaze away before I could see her. After our Grandpa's funeral, Lony and I both agreed that viewing the dead was creepy, and we wanted to be cremated. I tried to tell my mother this when she was driving me home from the hospital, but she'd kept her eyes on the road like she was all alone in the car. I probably should've let Grandma Nora know, since she was the one making most of the arrangements. Once I'd woken up and Mom didn't have to worry about me, she had to face Lony's death, and she slipped into a strange kind of depression, pretty much making her useless for anything other than staying in bed all day.

Our aunt presented us to our parents like china dolls to be inspected. Mom looked like someone had beaten her with a hammer and superglued her back together. Her navy blue suit, freshly blown out hair and make-up were perfect, but anyone could see all that was only a thin veneer barely holding the pieces of her together. She reached forward mechanically and straightened Aaron's tie. Her eyes reflected a glassy shine.

Dad stood shifting his weight from foot to foot as if his dress shoes were too tight. He drew me in next to him with a light squeeze on my shoulder. Once Aaron and I were between them like a buffer zone, the receiving line began moving again.

Thick grief washed over me with every new person who stood before me, making it difficult to breathe. I let my body shift into autopilot. While my arms hugged and my head bobbed in mute acknowledgment to the whispered words of sympathy, I shrank into myself and tried to fight off the urge to blow chunks all over my shoes. The line was insanely long, winding its way out the door, and after an hour, Dad let Aaron and I retreat upstairs to the family lounge to relax until the service started.

Away from the crowd, I finally felt like I could breathe again. I waited on a couch, letting a mug of coffee grow cold between my palms as various family members rotated in and out. My thirteen-year-old cousin, Geoffrey, sat in the corner playing Mario on his DS until Aunt Tina hustled him out with orders to talk to our great-aunts.

Aaron and I didn't speak. He sat across from me on another sofa with his eyes closed as if catching a cat-nap, although I could tell by the way he flinched whenever someone else entered the room, that he was wide awake.

When it was time for the memorial to start, our grandma came to fetch us. While my family is not religious, Grandma hired Bronwyn's father to hold the inter-faith service. As we entered the small chapel, I saw with horror that our front-row seats were situated directly in front of the casket. Panic hit me hard. I wasn't ready to see Lony. Somehow, seeing her body lying in that coffin would make her death official, and I wasn't ready for that. I didn't think I'd ever be ready for that. I swallowed hard and stared at my feet the whole way up the aisle. I discovered with immense relief once I sat down that my line of vision was low enough to prevent me from seeing inside the box.

Just before Pastor Tom began to speak, someone sank into the seat on the other side of Aaron. I looked down the row to see Cane Matthews. I'd forgotten all about him. My parents must have invited him to sit with the family. His face appeared to be carved out of stone, as if betrayal of the slightest emotion would cause the whole thing to crumble off his head.

The ceremony passed in a great rush, each second bringing me closer to having to say my final good-bye to my sister. While Pastor Tom talked, I fingered the vintage butterfly hair clip that I had stashed in my pocket. I'd found it a couple of years ago in a junk shop downtown. The wings were made of delicate sheets of abalone and tiny rhinestones formed the body. Lony was constantly stealing it from my jewelry box, leading to many arguments about how I should just give it to her since I rarely wore my hair up. The thing is I probably would've let her have it if she hadn't been so demanding about it. Instead, I held onto it out of spite. The clip now was fastened around a badly composed poem to my sister that I'd written in third grade. A few of the words were misspelled and the overly melodramatic lines didn't really rhyme, but Lony had kept it pinned to her bulletin board in her bedroom ever since. I planned to slip it and the hair clip into the casket before it was closed.

Aunt Tina gave the eulogy for the family. Grandma had asked me to do it, but I begged off. I didn't like public speaking on a good day, and there was no way I'd be able to hold it together on this one. My aunt's words washed over me without sinking in. My mind whirled with all of the things I wanted to say to Lony before they closed the casket on her forever. The last time I'd seen her, she and Cane had been bickering. I snuck a glance down the row at him. The muscles of his jaw twitched beneath the surface of his freshly shaven skin, and his blood-shot eyes appeared tired and dry. It was sad that her final moments had been spent fighting. When the eulogy was over, our family remained seated while ushers dismissed everyone else with instructions that the burial would be a private, family ceremony.

Once the bulk of the crowd cleared out of the chapel, our family members drifted up one at a time to kneel on the velvet cushion before the coffin to pay their last respects. I waited as long as possible. I didn't want an audience.

When my turn came, I settled on my knees beside her and folded my hands on the waxy wooden rail. Carefully, I allowed my gaze to drift over my sister from waist to head.

I had expected to see Lony there, but I realized with

some surprise that body lying there was not her. My sister was long gone. The mortician had made her up to appear younger and more conservative than she'd been in life. Her hair was brushed and positioned so that it framed her face. She wore the plum colored dress that we had taken our family pictures in the year before, a dress that I remembered her complaining made her neck itch. The smoky eye make-up that I'd been so accustomed to seeing on her over the past year was gone, leaving a fresh face with only a hint of mascara and lip gloss. It looked more like my body in the coffin than hers. I shuddered.

I'd been so absorbed with drinking in her appearance, I didn't notice the long moments that passed. When Dad touched my shoulder and indicated that my turn was up, my heart jumped into my throat. *No!* I screamed inside. *I'm not ready for her to be gone!*

Pastor Tom gathered the remaining family members and Cane in front of the coffin to say some last words. The tenor of his voice sounded far away, and I concentrated on saying my own silent good-byes, which I'd neglected to do before.

One by one, people began heading for their cars to get ready for the procession to the cemetery.

As I left the chapel, I turned back to see Cane, all alone now, watching the two somber men from the funeral home close the lid and set an arrangement of roses on top. He'd been the last person to see her in life. It seemed fitting that he be the last to see her in death.

It wasn't until we were in the car on the way home that I felt the butterfly hair clip still in my pocket.

# Chapter 8

THE NEXT WEEK and a half faded past me in blur. The pain in our house was almost unbearable. When Lony died, she left behind a hole that stifled us with its emptiness. My mother, Aaron and I spent most of our time in our bedrooms, Mom in a Valium-induced haze. She crumbled after the funeral and hadn't gotten out of her pajamas since. Aaron drowned his thoughts in death metal in the basement until Dad stopped by and told him to keep it down so as not to disturb Mom. Me? I spent long afternoons sitting on the cushy window seat in my bedroom watching a flock of cardinals nest in our backyard pine tree.

Just over two weeks after the accident, I awoke early to noise coming from the kitchen beneath me. I slid my arms into a Hawkeyes sweatshirt and wandered down to investigate. Aaron stood in front of the open refrigerator drinking milk from the carton. Mom would have yelled at him for it, but I never drank milk, so I didn't care.

"What are you doing?" I asked, leaning against the

51

counter. Aaron's blond hair was damp from the shower and he was dressed in jeans and a clean t-shirt which read "The ZOMBIE APOCALYPS is coming." I wasn't sure if it was advertising a band or making a social statement.

"What's it look like?" he grunted. "Going to school."

School. The thought of doing something as ordinary as going to school seemed foreign to me.

"Why?" I wondered.

Aaron flashed me a look like I was the stupidest girl he'd ever met. "It's Monday." He replaced the cap on the milk and slid it back into the refrigerator. His eyes drifted over me standing there barefoot and in pajamas. "You're not going?"

I shrugged. "I don't know. I guess I haven't thought about it."

Aaron's face softened and he nodded. "If you're not ready, you should stay home. But I . . . I just can't take this house anymore." He snatched up his bag from the table. "See ya."

I stood there for several minutes, my mind completely blank. It felt kind of nice standing alone, like being able to breathe fresh air after a long time in a stuffy room. For the first time since leaving the hospital, I got an urge to get out of the house, to go for a jog, to feel the sun on my skin. I wasn't ready to go back to class yet, but a run around the neighborhood sounded like it might be okay.

After swapping out my pj's for sweats, I walked down the hall to my mother's room to let her know I was going out. I opened her door slowly and peeked in. The shades were drawn tight, blocking out the morning sun. I could just make out a lump curled in a ball in the middle of the king-sized mattress. Aside from the funeral, my mom hadn't left her bed. The scent of unwashed sheets made my nose twitch.

Suddenly, my hands began to tremble and my stomach clenched. Intense sorrow hit me, seeming to radiate from the direction of the bed, both emotional and physical at the same time. It sunk into my body through my pores. My breath caught in my throat and something in my heart snapped. The void left from Lony's absence sucked the gravity right out of the room. I lost my grip on the door and dropped to the carpet. I hadn't realized I was sobbing until my mother's arms wrapped around me, rocking me side to side.

"I know, honey, I know," she whispered into my hair.

After school let out for the day, Bronwyn and Shawn stopped by to drop off some textbooks that I'd asked for. They had been at the funeral, but we didn't have much chance to talk. They both called regularly, but neither seemed to know what to say to me. I guess I understood that.

We exchanged big hugs as I invited them inside. Identical looks of horror crossed their faces at seeing my normally put-together mom standing barefoot in the kitchen wearing her dirty bathrobe and eating peaches directly out of a can with her fingers. What I saw as progress they probably saw as a scene from *Punked*. I herded them upstairs.

I moved a heap of discarded pajamas and t-shirts from my desk chair and dropped them on top of my already-full hamper, where at least half fell off onto the floor. Bronwyn took the chair while Shawn sprawled out in my window seat. He picked up my binoculars and looked through them.

"Spying on the neighbors?" he asked.

"Birds," I replied, then instantly felt stupid. I knew it sounded like a lame way to spend my time. "I've been watching the birds in the pines."

Bronwyn bit her lip as she tended to do when she was uncomfortable. "I don't think I've ever seen your room like this before," she commented, her eyes roaming around.

For the first time since I got home from the hospital, I really focused my attention on my surroundings. The bed was unmade and the sheets were loose and wrinkled from tossing and turning. Several dirty dishes with clumps of caked-on food were stacked on the desk like my own personal Leaning Tower of Pisa. Next to the dishes, the photos from my bulletin board lay in a crumpled heap from where I'd ripped them down in a moment of rage and regret. On the floor in front of the closet was a pile of old school papers that I'd pulled out of my nightstand drawers for some reason late one night, and never bothered putting back.

"You were always the neat one," Bronwyn whispered.

"Well, now I'm the *only* one," I snapped. Bronwyn cringed and gnawed at her lip again. My harsh tone shocked me as much as her, and I immediately felt sorry.

"Cady," Shawn said, walking over and wrapping his arms around me "She didn't mean anything bad. Don't get angry. We're just worried about you."

I allowed myself the luxury of sinking into his skinny, yet strangely comforting, chest. A wave of calm coated me like a blanket. "I'm so sorry," I sighed.

Bronwyn slid up behind me and joined our embrace. The calming sensation intensified and the tense muscles in my shoulders relaxed. Sandwiched between my friends was the best I'd felt since before my Dad left.

"I don't have to be home for a couple of hours," Bronwyn said, "Why don't you let Shawn and I help you clean up?"

I groaned. I wasn't in the mood to clean, but I was willing to concede that doing something productive might make me feel better. I nodded.

Bronwyn gathered all of the dirty clothes and the sheets off of my bed and dragged them off to the laundry room, while Shawn helped me make up the bed with clean linens. When we carried my dirty dishes downstairs, I noticed the heap already sitting in the sink and stacked on the countertops, the remnants of what couldn't be stuffed into the dish washer. It didn't look like anyone had run a load since the accident.

Bronwyn and I tackled the kitchen while Shawn ran the vacuum, first in my bedroom and then through the rest of the house. My mother, holed up in her bedroom, didn't come out of her room to help.

By the time Bronwyn had to leave to get ready for her Bible study group, the house was more or less put to order. I hugged both of my friends tightly and watched as they trotted off to Shawn's Toyota parked across the street. As they drove away, my energy left with them, replaced by dull emptiness.

Returning to my newly cleaned bedroom, I sank down on the plush cushion of my window seat, feeling a little like a balloon that just had the air let out. My hands automatically picked up my dad's old pair of binoculars from his time in the Army. The cardinals looked like they were redecorating their nest. I wondered if they applied the same Feng Shui principles my mother did. Wouldn't want to see their Chi off balance.

A smudge of color appeared in the background, and I readjusted my focus. It was my neighbor, stooped over in her herb garden clipping leaves and dropping them into a pouch at her waist. I didn't know her name. We had adjoining backyards, but her house faced the next street over. The woman had moved in a year ago after our old neighbor died. My mother frequently complained about how poorly this one kept her yard. The garden took up almost half of the space, the bushy plants over-grown and planted haphazardly. The back half of the yard, the half which reached all the way up to our chain link fence, was a large patch of grass which had not been mowed once since the woman moved in, like an urban haven for all kinds of woodland creatures.

I trained the binoculars on her face. The woman rarely came outside, so I was curious to get a look. She was younger than her long baggy dresses led me to believe. Auburn hair cascaded down her back in wavy tangles as if she hadn't bothered to brush it that morning. She wore no makeup, but was exceptionally pretty with a smooth, creamy complexion. A slight smile rested on her lips as she clipped away like she might have been having a silent conversation with herself.

Zooming the focus out, I captured her whole body in my view. Her clothes were weird. I'd noticed them before in the glimpses over the past year. She favored long flowing skirts layered over each other in a way that my mother would have called Bohemian. Her top was a simple, long-sleeved t-shirt in bright blue. I was thinking of zooming in on her house when the woman glanced up and looked right at me. Her face broke into a toothy grin and her hand raised in a little wave.

I shot out of my window, dropping the binoculars on the carpet, embarrassed to have been caught spying. Oh, well. It was time to do something more productive than stare at birds anyway.

The text books that Shawn had brought sat in a neat stack on my desk. Just the thought of school overwhelmed me and made my palms sweat. I'd already missed eleven days in a row. Neither of my parents had mentioned anything about me going back. The doctors at the hospital advised them I should take it slow and suggested a therapist who specialized in post traumatic stress disorder. I had an appointment scheduled for Wednesday.

I carried the school books over to the bed and opened my literature text. A blue envelope baring Ms. Crowell's loopy handwriting on the front dropped out from beneath the cover. I opened it to find a sympathy card with a little note inside.

*"Words can't express how deeply sorry I am for your loss. I know school is the last thing on your mind, but you might find it helpful to focus on something else for a while. I marked a few pages in the poetry section that you might find comforting. I've also enclosed a list of assignments that you've missed. Don't worry about the due dates, just do the best you can. If you need any help, please feel free to contact me anytime."*

On the bottom, Ms. Crowell listed both her home and cell phone numbers. I ran my finger over the digits. I had only been in her class for a week before the accident, not nearly long enough to decide whether I liked her as a teacher or not. Somehow, that handwritten note with her phone numbers meant more to me than any of the hundreds of sympathy cards we'd accumulated since the funeral.

Maybe Ms. Crowell was right. I needed something more than a family of cardinals to distract my mind. Reviewing the assignment list, I noticed the class had already moved on from the Greeks and had skipped ahead to the Elizabethans. I heaved a sigh of relief at seeing we were to read A Midsummer Night's Dream. I'd watched the movie on television once and liked it well enough. I couldn't have handled reading one of Shakespeare's tragedies. I flipped open the thick book and began reading.

I'd just gotten to the point where Nick Bottom's head was turned into a donkey when the land-line phone rang. Probably Dad checking in on me again.

"Hello?" I answered, my eyes still half-reading the page.

There was a long pause before the caller spoke. "Uh, may I speak to Arcadia please?" His voice was soft and unsure, not familiar to me at all.

"This is Cady," I replied.

"Hi. This is Bryan . . . Bryan Sullivan . . . you know, the new kid."

It took me a moment to place the name. When I did, my belly did a little flip. "Oh, right, from literature class."

I sat up straight on my bed. Boys called the house all the time, but other than Shawn, they had usually wanted to talk to Lony.

"I hope you don't mind my calling. Are you busy? Do you feel up to talking?"

I shoved Ms. Crowell's card between the pages to keep my place. "No . . . I mean, yeah . . . it's cool. I was just catching up on some homework, but I could use a break. How'd you get my number?"

"Phone book." He paused and took an audible breath in and out. "Listen, I'm really sorry about your sister. I actually went to the funeral, but you looked sort of overwhelmed with people, so I didn't come up and say anything."

"Oh . . ." I don't know what surprised me more, that I hadn't noticed him or that he'd been there at all. "Told you I'm not very observant."

"Well, you had a good excuse."

We both went quiet for an awkward moment. A faint metallic taste touched my tongue. I realized I was gnawing the chapped skin on my lower lip.

"So, um . . . how's school going?" I asked. Lame, I know.

"It's good, I guess. I mean, it's school. If it weren't at least a little emotionally damaging, they wouldn't be doing their job, right?"

"Right." I squeezed my eyes tightly and willed myself to come up with something to say that wouldn't make me seem like a complete moron.

"So, do you know when you're going to come back yet?"

"No idea. My brother, Aaron, went back today, but he hasn't been home yet, so I haven't asked him how it went." I picked at the pilled fabric of my bedspread. "I don't know how to tell if I'm ready to face it again, and my parents have been like zero help."

"I understand. Actually, that's why I'm calling." Bryan paused as if gathering the courage to say something. "Um . . . my older brother . . . Jesse? He passed away last year. Thought you might like to talk to someone who's been there, you know?"

"Didn't you tell me that you're an only child?"

"I am . . . *now* I am. After Jesse died, my parents thought we should be closer to our extended family in the Midwest. My mother's side. So when my dad scored a job transfer to Dubuque, they couldn't pack us off fast enough."

"Oh. How . . . how did Jesse . . . ?" My tongue stumbled over the question.

"Die? Do you know what hemophilia is?"

"Some kind of blood disease, right?"

"Yeah. It's a genetic disorder where the blood can't clot very well. A cut or a bruise can be fatal if doctors can't get the bleeding to stop in time. Anyway, Jesse was snowboarding —something he was absolutely forbidden to do because of his condition. He was always doing stupid things he shouldn't. The slope wasn't even all that dangerous; he just banked too hard on a curve and tumbled into a tree. He was able to get up and walk back to the lodge, but by the time he got there, a huge bruise had formed on his side and began spreading across his back."

"Oh, no," I whispered.

"Yeah. His friends drove him to the nearest hospital, but he'd lost consciousness before they arrived. He died before my parents could get there. I guess he'd torn his liver when he fell."

I squeezed my eyes tightly. Even hearing about the death of a boy I didn't know could bring me to tears. "I'm so sorry, Bryan."

He sighed on the other end of the phone as if he were forcing himself to be strong. "It's okay. I mean, it was hard at first —it's still hard —but it gets easier. I wanted you to know that. It gets easier."

My chest tightened and my skin warmed for what seemed like the first time in days. "Thank you, Bryan. It means so much to me that you called. It's like no one really understands what it's like to lose a sibling. My friends have tried to help, but they've never experienced anything even close."

"Have you been able to talk with your family?"

"Yeah, right! My mother has banned my father from the house and won't let me go over to his place. And she's been in a Valium haze since the funeral. My brother and I are spending all of our time in our bedrooms on opposite ends of the house. It's like we brought the mortuary home with us."

"I saw your brother today, at school. He looked like a guy walking in a dream. I thought maybe you would've come back, too."

"I don't think I'm ready yet. It just seems so hard. I can't stop thinking about her as it is. How will I be able to look at her locker or her table in the lunch room or the cheerleaders walking around in their uniforms without thinking of her?"

"You can't. You're gonna see Lony everywhere for a while. It will totally suck . . . but that's okay."

"No! It's not okay!" Tears were spilling down my face in earnest now. "These reminders just make the hole she left in my life bigger. She was my sister . . . my *twin*! All of my life we were defined by our relationship to each other. Lony's the outgoing one, and I'm the introverted one. She's got the style, and I've got the brains. She's liked by all of the boys, and I'm liked by all the teachers. I don't even know who I am without her!"

Bryan stayed silent for a few minutes while I sobbed. When I calmed down, I set the receiver down to wipe my face blow my nose with a wad of tissues.

I picked the phone back up and cradled it into the crease of my neck. "I'm sorry, Bryan. I didn't mean to lose it. I'm doing that a lot lately."

"Cady, don't apologize," he said. His voice was as soothing as hot chocolate. "Don't ever apologize for what you are feeling. I understand."

I sniffed again and asked, "So with Jesse . . . how did you move beyond it? I mean, how did you go on with your life?"

"Well, it sounds cliché, but I took it one day at a time.

I got back into my routine, you know, going to school, doing my homework. I had a few close friends who helped me along. They kept me busy, but didn't get offended when I didn't have as good of a time as they did."

"What about your family?"

"My mom also was lost for a while, but she pulled herself out of it after a few weeks. My dad . . . well, he doesn't show his emotions much. I never even saw him cry, which seems weird, but if you knew my dad, it's not a shocker. He went back to work the day after the funeral like nothing even happened. I don't think my mother has forgiven him for that yet. They're not talking a whole lot anymore. I suspect this move is a last-ditch effort on keeping their marriage together. It's weird living in a house where no one speaks to each other. Sometimes I wish they would just separate and get it over with."

"I know what you mean there. My dad had actually moved out the day before Lony's accident."

"Whoa! Brutal."

I pulled a blanket out of my closet and carried it over to the window seat where I curled up all cozy-like with the phone. Bryan and I talked for over an hour. I told him about my upcoming therapy appointment, and he told me about the psychologist that his mother made him go see after Jesse's death and what I might expect.

"So," he said finally, "I have to go. My father will be home soon and my mother has dinner almost ready. Will I see you in school tomorrow?"

I could tell by the way he asked it that he thought it was time I get back in the swing of things, but didn't want to pressure me.

"I don't know, Bryan. I don't know if I can walk in

there. Everyone is going to stare at me." I knew I sounded whiney, but didn't care.

"Tell you what . . . I'll pick you up in the morning and walk in with you."

"Seriously? You'd do that? Why? I mean, you barely know me."

He paused as if weighing his words. "Like I said, I've been there. And, since you're one of the few people who has spoken to me outside of class since moving here, it's my way of thanking you. You can always go home early if it gets to be too much."

I thought about it for a moment. I was going to have to go back sometime. Aaron did it. I guess it was my turn.

"You don't have to come get me."

"I want to. Just tell me where you live."

I had to admit to myself, having someone there for support would be nice. For some reason, this total stranger was able to comfort me in ways my family and friends had not. Part of it, of course, was because of Bryan's experience with his brother, but I think the other part was because he never really knew Lony. He had nothing to compare me to, unlike other kids at school. Bryan saw me as a whole person and not as a half of a matched set.

"Okay. I'll give it a shot."

I gave Bryan my address and was ready to hang up when I thought of something. "Wait a sec. Before, you said that your brother's hemophilia was genetic . . ."

"Yes. It is passed by females and carried by males. My mother is a carrier. She passed it down. I have hemophilia, too."

# Chapter 9

I COULDN'T SLEEP that night. After my conversation with Bryan, I waited for Aaron to come home so I could ask him about his day. It was past ten before I heard his truck pull into the driveway and he slipped quietly down to his bedroom before I could catch him.

In the morning, my head was a fuzzy mess of cobwebs, and my eyes were dry and red. I hadn't slept well. After showering, I wasted over a half hour trying on and taking off clothes, unable to make a decision about what to wear to school. When I saw how late the time was I yanked on a pair of faded Levi's and a long-sleeved t-shirt. My stomach felt acidic and queasy. I gulped down an Eggo waffle, but it sat in my belly like a rock. I thought about poking my head into Mom's room to tell her where I was going —I hadn't seen her at all the previous evening —but remembering the wall of depression that had overcome me the day before when I went in her room, I decided to just leave a note for her on the counter.

The doorbell rang. I scooped up my heavy backpack and opened the door. Bryan stood on the stoop, leaning his lanky frame against a post. Time must have faded his image in my mind, because the guy standing before me, grinning with one up-turned corner of his mouth, was gorgeous! The dark of his eyes and hair were accented by a pair of black plastic framed glasses, making him appear studious, but cool at the same time. He radiated calm and strength, but also a hint of nervousness. My shoulders relaxed and I responded with an echoing grin.

"You're wearing glasses," I commented.

"Only when I drive," he replied. "Ready?"

I nodded and pulled the door closed behind me.

We drove the couple of blocks to school. His car was a older model Lexus, a little nicer than the average high school student. We didn't talk much. The air between us felt thick and awkward. He tapped his long fingers on the steering wheel, and I knew he was as anxious as I was.

Bryan found a parking space in the middle of the lot. He shut the ignition off, but neither of us made a move to exit the vehicle. He removed his glasses and folded them into a case which he then tossed up onto the dashboard. My chest tightened with nerves, and I drummed my fingers rapidly on my leg. It was only a few minutes before the bell and students, alone and in groups, made their way purposefully to the doors.

"Maybe I shouldn't have made you do this," Bryan said. "You don't have to go in. I can take you back home if you want."

"You're not making me do this. And as tempting as it is to go back to bed, getting back to regular life is the best thing to do." I took a deep breath and let it out with a shudder. "I'm just glad I don't have to do it alone."

Bryan's expression softened and he reached over to pat the back of my hand. For a second, I thought he might take hold of it, causing me to suck in a quick breath. But he didn't. The touch was gone as quickly as it was given.

"Let's go," he said as he retrieved his bag from the backseat and opened the door.

My head grew dizzy as I climbed out into the crisp morning air. My stomach ached. The bell rang as we were approaching the building, but Bryan was content to let me walk at my own pace, without hurry. He accompanied me all the way to my government class. I could hear Mr. Steele in the classroom taking roll.

"Thanks, Bryan," I said. "I really appreciate your help."

He patted my shoulder stiffly. "I'll be right here when you get out of class."

"You don't need to walk me to all of my classes," I said with a nervous chuckle.

"I know I don't have to, but my American history class is just two doors down. No big deal."

Bryan lifted his hand in a wave and strutted off down the hall. I waited until he disappeared into his classroom. As soon as he turned the corner out of sight, my fear came back. Roll call was over, and the principal's voice poured out of the intercom speakers for the morning announcements. I thought I might be able to slip into my seat before anyone noticed. I was wrong.

As I rounded the doorway to sneak down the aisle, I bumped into the metal garbage can, knocking it over with a clunk on the hard tiles. Twenty-one heads looked up at once. Upon recognizing me, their collective eyes shot down to the tops of their desks. The tension in the room jumped up so sharply, my lungs constricted. Suddenly, my neck broke out in a cold sweat, and my cheeks flared. I leaned over to right the garbage can and my bag slid off my shoulder, breaking the strap with the weight of too many textbooks.

"Good morning, Cady," Mr. Steele said, picking up his attendance book to mark me present. "Class, pay attention to the announcements."

The students turned back toward the front. I clutched the broken strap of my bag and slid into my third-row seat.

I remembered nothing of the teacher's lecture. Instead, I obsessed over my discomfort. It was hard to describe, but the room felt nervous . . . twitchy with my presence. It wasn't like anything I'd ever felt before. Several times I felt eyes watching me, but when I glanced around, all I saw were kids bent over their papers, scribbling notes or doodling in the margins. *Paranoid much?*

I jumped when the shrill bell rang out, ending first period. I really needed to chill out. I shook my head at my idiocy and stepped into the river of teenagers flowing up and down the hallway.

Someone touched my arm just above the elbow. I looked up to see Bryan. He smiled and asked, "How was it?"

I glanced around and noticed people looking at me as they passed by. "Awkward."

"Well, awkward is okay. You know you can do it now. With each class, it'll get easier."

We merged into the traffic walking left. I wanted to stop at my locker to drop off the broken bag and the textbooks that I wouldn't need. The crowd of students felt more oppressive than it ever had before. Flickers of hot and cold brushed my body, causing a sheen of cold sweat to dampen my skin. I felt my forehead, but didn't detect a fever, just a dull ache forming between my eyes.

When we rounded the corner, I felt like someone socked me in the chest with a baseball bat. Before me was Lony's locker, looking as if Hallmark threw up all over it. Photos and cards were taped in over-lapping layers so no metal was exposed. What didn't make it on the locker itself leaned neatly along the base of the wall. A vase with wilting roses stood on the floor with a hand-made sign sticking out which read, "Gone to the angels." Teddy-bears and Beanie Babies with blank eyes and mocking smiles stared up at me from the floor.

"Oh, my god . . ." I whispered, my face draining to white. Kids passing by between classes stared at me, making my skin crawl.

Bryan clutched my arm and steered me into an empty classroom. "I'm so sorry, Cady."

"What is that? A shrine?" I shouted, my voice breaking like a twelve-year-old boy. I started to hyperventilate, the air in my lungs heaving in and out, in and out.

Bryan pulled me into his arms, his hand patting my hair. My tears soaked into the cotton of his White Stripes t-shirt, leaving dark gray blotches.

"I'm so sorry. I had no idea that was there. I never come down this hallway."

I didn't wrap my arms around him; rather I drew them in tightly to my sides, my fists balled up clutching his shirt. I hadn't noticed how cold I was until I was snuggling against him, basking in his body heat. Maybe I should have been embarrassed, but at that moment, all I could focus on was his calm warmth. He could have been anyone, I just needed to be held.

"It's okay, Cady," he whispered. "You stay here. I'll go

get the janitor to take it all away."

As soon as he drew away, an irrational wave of anger rolled through me that even Bryan's calming influence couldn't touch.

"How could they? Don't they realize she was *my* sister? That my locker is right there, too? It's bad enough I have to live down the hall from her empty bedroom. Do they expect me to step around that —that *altar* between every class?"

A small rational part of me knew I was being a bitch, that those students lost someone too, but my emotions were out of control with selfish need. I started pacing and Bryan just stepped back and watched.

Mr. Small, the computer arts teacher, poked his head in to see what all the shouting was about.

"Oh, Miss Day! Is everything all right?" He snatched a box of tissues from the window sill and held them out to me as if he didn't want to come too close.

"It's fine," Bryan assured him, "She just wasn't prepared to see that memorial at her sister's locker."

"Oh, well . . . I guess I can call the custodian and have it removed."

"Forget it!" I said. "I'll do it myself."

Before they could stop me, I went out into the hallway and plucked a poem off of the metal. It was some sappy thing that struggled to rhyme. I ripped it and let the pieces float to my feet. I could feel the eyes of the crowd on my back, boring into my skull. A cold cloud of grief wafted around me. Without realizing it, my fingers started ripping the pictures and notes stuck to the locker with Scotch tape. My pinky ran along the edge of a Post-It which read "I'll miss you," slicing a tiny, painful cut in my skin. As I was shaking my hand, my foot knocked over the vase of flowers, spilling gunky water and soaking the largest of the teddy-bears.

Around me, kids stopped and stared, ignoring Mr. Small's pleas for them to keep moving. Murmurs wrapped around me, "Whoa! Cady's losing it." "Think we should try to help?" "I miss Lony too, but what a drama queen!" Their anger blended with mine until I shivered and all I could see was red. I tore at a photo of Lony standing in her cheerleader uniform, her pom-poms in the air as she stood on the shoulders of her teammates. When it was shredded beyond recognition, I moved on to a group shot of Lony and Cane with a bunch of their friends piled on top of each other on a couch in some anonymous basement rec room. The confetti of Kodak paper fluttered to the floor like a ticker-tape parade.

Bryan placed a tentative hand on my shoulder. His touch poked a hole in my anger, letting it diffuse, slowly, until it was gone altogether. My fingers stopped frozen in mid-rip. I looked down at the mess around my feet. My jaw dropped and my wild eyes latched onto his in shame. Just as my knees gave out, Bryan caught me and lowered me to the floor in a heap of limbs. He pulled me onto his lap and turned my sobbing face into the crook of his neck to shield me from our nosey classmates staring and whispering excitedly. The disdain they felt for me was tangible. The bell rang for second period, and a few more teachers arrived to usher everyone along to their classes.

I couldn't look at the mess. My body curled up and huddled into Bryan's as if I could make myself small enough to disappear. He stroked my hair and rocked me gently.

A janitor in a denim uniform showed up with a push broom and a large, rubber garbage can. He waited off to the side quietly, unable to clear the mess away with us sitting in the middle of it.

Once the hall was mostly empty of students, Mr. Small crouched down and whispered something to Bryan.

I felt his head bob in a nod. "I'll take her home now." Bryan bent his mouth to my ear. "Let's get you out of here."

As Bryan helped me to my feet, I caught a pair of green eyes, blazing with molten hatred staring right at me, causing my body to jerk in shock. Cane Matthews stood across the hall. It was the first time I'd seen him since the funeral. His face appeared to have aged, gray smudges spread beneath his eyes and his jaw clenched tightly. He bent down and picked up a torn photograph of Lony that had been taken over the summer at cheerleading camp. His gaze softened slightly on the photo, but when he looked at me again, I felt a stab in my gut. The icy pain rolled off Cane so thickly the air felt like water, making my lungs heave for breath. I shivered uncontrollably.

Bryan relieved me of the broken backpack without a word, took my hand. "Ignore him. Come on." He steered me toward the doors.

I felt Cane's glare on my back the whole way down the hall and out the front doors.

Bryan offered to stay with me, but I made him go back to school. I spent the rest of the day in my pj's huddled in bed with the covers over my head.

The doorbell rang around 3:00, but neither my mother nor I made a move to answer it. Just after dark, I woke from a nap to someone knocking on my bedroom door.

"Can I come in?" Aaron's guff voice called from the hall outside.

I yanked the covers down from the tent I had made with my pillows to block out the harsh afternoon sunlight.

"Yeah," I croaked. "Come in."

Aaron stepped into the room and glanced around. It had been a long time since he had been in my bedroom. My brother and I have never been very close. He was only fourteen months older, but he'd always held himself apart from us. I'm not sure if that was because we were girls or because he felt excluded by our twin-ness.

He didn't turn on the light, just wandered over and sat down by my feet.

"I heard what happened this morning."

"I don't know why I freaked out like that," I groaned.

Aaron nodded in sympathy. In the light emanating from the hallway, I could see dark smudges under his lower lashes and hollowness in his cheeks. All at once I felt guilty for not being there more for him. I hadn't given much thought to the fact that he also lost a sister. My hand snaked out from beneath my peppermint-colored comforter and squeezed his. After a moment, he squeezed back.

"I would have warned you about the locker if I'd known you were going to go to school this morning. I couldn't look at it either."

"I shouldn't have flipped out like that. Lony had tons of friends. They have a right to mourn her the way they need to."

Aaron just bobbed his head and mashed his lips together.

"How are you, Aaron? Do you want to talk about it?"

He let out a whoosh of air. "Oh, I don't know, Cady. I imagine I'm feeling about like you are right now; sadness, anger —mostly at myself for not spending more time with her —with you both. And then this house . . . I've been kind of thinking about going to stay with Dad for a while."

"Have you told Mom yet?"

"Are you kidding?" He said with a raised eye brow, the metal bar through it glinting in the low light. "She's so doped up there's no talking to her. I don't think she's taken a shower since the funeral. Besides, she probably wouldn't even notice if I left."

I didn't know what to say. In the space of only a few weeks, our family as we knew it changed into something from a bad after-school special.

"I'd like to go see Dad tomorrow," I said. "Think you want to come with me?"

"Sure," he replied.

We lapsed into silence, nothing more to say. He clung to me with one hand and picked at the cuticle of his thumb with the other. Eventually, he stood up and shuffled toward the door.

Just before entering the hallway, Aaron turned back to me, his face framed in the backlight. "Think you want to try school again tomorrow?"

I shook my head. "I don't think I'm ready yet."

He nodded once in agreement. "Okay. I'll pick you up when I'm done and we can go to Dad's. Want the door closed?"

"Yeah."

Aaron left, pulling the door shut behind him. I flopped back onto my mattress. My down pillow had grown flat over the two weeks of near constant use. I yanked it out from beneath me to fluff it up. The phone started ringing. I checked the caller ID before answering. It was Bryan.

"So . . ." he hedged, "I've been sitting here for an hour debating with myself over whether I should call or not. If you don't want to talk, that's cool, but I at least need to know you are not sitting in the dark listening to Leonard Cohen music and contemplating banishing yourself to a European boarding school."

I grinned for the first time all day. It felt good.

"In the dark yes, but no Cohen."

"And you're not going to runaway to Switzerland, because right now, you are like the only friend I have here. Selfish, I know, but I am a teenager after all."

"No Switzerland, I promise. It gets really cold there, and I don't ski."

We talked for a while about nothing. He never mentioned how my flip-out was talked about at school, but I'm sure even a boy with no friends would have heard the gossip bantered around. Before we hung up, I'd decided to work from home for the rest of the week and I'd start back to school fresh on Monday.

# Chapter 10

THE NEXT MORNING, I woke early to the sound of tweeting cardinals. I peered through the binoculars and watched them flit from branch to branch around their nests. I kind of felt sorry for the females who appeared dull and brown compared to the royal red of their mates. I guess I knew what it was like to live in someone else's glow. *Emo, much?*

I tossed the binoculars down on my window seat and stretched my arms up tall. I had to get out of the house. The sun was shining outside, and the constant throb of depression in my house was threatening to pull me under again. I showered, dressed and went out to the Honda Civic that I had shared with Lony. My Fallulah CD blared from the stereo, and I sung along off-key. I swung through a McDonald's drive through for a yogurt parfait before heading out to Dubuque County Animal Sanctuary, located on the north edge of town.

Dr. Kristy Fineman's face lit up when she saw me walk

in the door. Bronwyn and I started volunteering at the shelter the summer after eighth grade. Last year, Dr. Kristy put us on the payroll. It was only ten hours a week at minimum wage, but I loved animals so much that I would've continued working for nothing.

"Cady!" The thin woman in a white doctor's coat rounded the corner of the reception desk to draw me into a big hug. Dr. Kristy and her husband, Mark, were both at the funeral, but I hadn't seen them since. "It's so good to see you!"

"Don't squish my breakfast," I said snatching the paper bag out from between us. "Well, I think I can handle dogs better than my classmates today, so thought I'd come in for a few hours."

Dr. Kristy drew back and checked me over thoughtfully as if I were one of her patients. Faint crow's feet lined the corners of her eyes; giving the impression her face was a perpetual smile.

"Well, I know Murphy will be glad to see you."

Murphy was a goofy Labrador with large floppy feet and one ear that stuck up in the air. Dr. Kristy's brother owned him, but he traveled a lot for work, so he kennels Murphy here at the shelter frequently.

"I just want to eat my breakfast, and then I can take a group out for a walk."

"No problem," Dr. Kristy replied, patting my arm. "I have a few appointments this morning, and then Gina is going to assist me on a couple neuters. Sarah will be here soon to watch the desk."

I carried my breakfast into the break room where I poured myself a cup of Columbian brew from the pot on the counter and ate. When I finished, I set out on my rounds of checking the cat cages. I filled food and water dishes, scooped the litter boxes and wiped down the interiors. The kitties wound themselves around my ankles rubbing their faces on my pant legs. I scratched each set of ears before depositing them back into their cages.

When I finished giving the cats some love, I walked out back to the dog kennels. A cacophony of excited barks and whines greeted my arrival. There were two long rows of high-fenced enclosures with metal roofs that rumbled like rocket engines when it rained. The shelter also had indoor kennels for overnights and two large paddocks where dogs could run and play in groups. I walked up and down the row greeting and petting the dogs I recognized and introducing myself to the new arrivals by letting them sniff my fist. Murphy spotted me approaching the enclosure where he lounged with a gray bulldog named Tank and Dr. Kristy's terrier mutt called Lucy, who came to work with the doc every day. The happy lab leaped to his feet and stood on his hind legs, paws on the fence and tongue dangling happily from his mouth.

"Hey, Murph! How's my boy?" I said as I unlocked the gate and entered the enclosure. The three dogs swarmed around my legs yipping and doing the puppy two-step for attention. I petted each of them in turn, before fastening their leashes and leading them out to the trails behind the shelter.

Dr. Kristy and Mark had inherited the three hundred acre farm a few years back from some relative. Uninterested in farming, they leveled the dilapidated farm buildings, constructed the shelter and clinic, and created walking trails which twisted through the woods and over-grown pasture land.

The three dogs and I strolled along the dirt path, the noise of the forest humming around us. Tank strained at his leash, wanting to chase squirrels, and then pouted when I wouldn't let him loose. As we approached a rocky incline, I scooped up Lucy to carry her. It was then that I discovered something odd.

Running my hand along Lucy's velvet belly, I felt a buzzing coldness radiating out from her compact body. It made my palm prick and tingle. Something tickled in the back of my mind, something bad.

I set the dog down. She stared up at me with her pointed nose. She didn't appear different than she did any other day. Quickly wrapping Murphy's and Tank's leashes around the branches of a low bush, I knelt down next to Lucy. My fingers trailed the markings of her brindled fur. Just under the ribcage on her right side I felt the hum vibrating strongest. Cold floated up from the spot, so that even with my hand six inches above it, my fingers quivered. Some instinct inside me was telling me the dog was in pain, which made no sense at all. Lucy appeared completely normal. When I touched the cold spot on her side there was something distinctly foreign about whatever was inside of her. That thought nagged at the base of my skull, and I grew anxious.

Cupping Lucy's muzzle, I stared deep into her golden-brown eyes. They were as clear and bright as any other day, but I was convinced something was gravely wrong. I scooped Lucy up in my arms, yanked the other two leashes free from the bush and rushed the pack back to the clinic.

My chest was huffing and sweat dampened my body by the time I made it to the yard. I'd run most of the way, only slowing enough to accommodate Tank's short stride.

My fingers fumbled with the kennel keys, but the lock clicked open easily. I rushed Tank and Murphy inside, not stopping to remove the leashes from their collars. With Lucy still in my arms, I hurried to find Dr. Kristy.

The doctor had changed into her surgery scrubs and stood in her office going over charts with her assistant, Gina. Their faces shot up in surprise when I bounded into the room holding Lucy out toward them.

"What is it, Cady?" Dr. Kristy asked, her brow heightened in surprise. "Is something wrong?"

I nodded and set Lucy down on her desk. "Feel...her..." I huffed, trying to catch my breath. "Here." I took the doctor's cool hand and placed it on the vibrating spot on the dog's chest. "Do you feel it?"

"Feel what?" she asked. Both doctor and dog stared at me like I was nuts.

"There's something there. In her chest," I insisted. "Right here!"

Dr. Kristy patted Lucy down, checking her bones, palpitating her organs. "I don't feel anything."

"That's because it's under the rib cage," I explained. "On her lung."

Dr. Kristy exchanged a glance with Gina, who stepped forward and began feeling around also.

"I don't feel anything, either," Gina confirmed.

"Please!" I insisted. "You have to believe me! Something's in there and it's bad!"

I started pacing in circles, trying to find a way for them to understand. The truth was I didn't know myself how I knew Lucy had a lung problem —I just did. I was as sure of it as I was my own name.

"Cady, maybe you should sit down," Dr. Kristy said in a calm, compassionate voice that agitated my fragile nerves.

"Don't do that!" I pleaded. "Don't patronize me! Don't talk to me like I'm losing it. You know how much I love these animals, right? Do you think I would lie to you? Would

I make up something that could be harmful to Lucy?"

Both the doctor and Gina shook their heads.

"Just take some x-rays and look. It doesn't hurt to look."

Dr. Kristy thought about it for a moment before replying, "Okay. I'll take a look. Gina, can you help me check Lucy out?"

I knew she was only doing it to humor me, to appease the grieving girl, but I didn't care. I knew deep down in my gut that there was something in Lucy that shouldn't be there.

The doctor picked the jolly terrier up off the desk. "Cady, you can go back to work. I'll come get you as soon as I finish with Lucy."

I reluctantly returned to the kennel to remove the leashes from Tank and Murphy. In the few minutes that I'd been gone, Tank had managed to drag his through his water bowl, soaking it.

"It's okay, boys," I whispered, patting them both on their sides. "Lucy's going to be okay. Dr. Kristy's on the case."

I tried to busy myself filling water dishes and sweeping out kennels, but my heart wasn't in it. I wanted to know what was wrong with Lucy. My head snapped up when the clinic door opened. Gina was waving at me.

"Come 'ere," she called before turning back inside. I dropped the broom to the ground and rushed in to find her and the doctor examining black and white scans against a backlight on the wall.

Dr. Kristy's lips were tight, and a deep line formed between her pencil-thin brows. She cast me an odd glance at my entrance.

"Cady, come look at this," she said, pointing to the picture with the end of a pen.

I stepped forward to see the skeletal outline of Lucy's

torso. The white ribs curved gracefully, protecting the precious cargo within. Even with my un-trained eyes, the white blurry mass in the lower-right lung was obvious. Dr. Kristy's head shook from side to side as if she were having an internal debate and losing.

"What is it?" I asked.

"Some kind of tumor," she answered. Her voice was distracted. After a silent moment, she turned and looked at me with puzzlement. "How did you know Lucy had a tumor on her lung? I didn't notice any symptoms."

My cheeks reddened, and I stared at her blankly. "I don't know. I guess I just . . . felt it."

"How did you feel it? The mass is beneath the ribs. It's not detectible from her exterior."

My mouth dropped open dumbly. How could I tell her about the buzzing, about the coldness and the vibrations that apparently only I could feel?

"Gina, can you give us a moment?" the doctor asked, then gestured for me to sit.

Once we were alone, Dr. Kristy slipped her glasses off and gave me that serious expression that adults give when they are trying to get you to level with them.

"I'm just trying to get a better understanding, because without your detection, Lucy might be in serious jeopardy. She still might be, but because of you, at least I know to go in and remove the mass. Cady, can you tell me what exactly you felt?"

Dr. Kristy was the adult I trusted most, even more than my parents sometimes.

"I'm not trying to be difficult, honest. It's just hard for me to describe."

"Can you try?"

I nodded and began to tell her exactly what happened from the time I set off down the trail with the dogs to when I realized something was wrong with Lucy.

"It was like this cold glow that vibrated off of the spot. The feeling would get stronger, more concentrated, the closer my hand got to the bottom of her right lung. Then, some —instinct, maybe? —told me that there was something in her that shouldn't be there. I just *knew*."

The doctor gazed at me thoughtfully, her head bobbing slowly as she took in my words.

"Has this ever happened before?" she asked.

I shook my head. "No. Never. It was weird."

She sighed. "Well, I need to go help Gina prep for surgery. We have to wait until tomorrow for Lucy, since she's eaten today. I don't know how you did it, but thank you."

Dr. Kristy gathered her things and left the office. I sat there chewing my thumb nail down to the quick.

# Chapter 11

A FTER LEAVING THE shelter, I called my dad to see if Aaron and I could stop by, but there was some sort of crisis on one of his job sites that would keep him working until well into the night. I could tell he felt bad putting me off. We hadn't spent much time together since the funeral. I suspected he was using work as a distraction from dwelling on his loss. I guess we all cope in our own way. I sent Aaron a text to cancel our plans.

At home, my brother and his friend, Trent, were hanging out in the kitchen waiting for a frozen pizza to heat up in the toaster oven. Aaron sat on top of the counter tossing an oven mitt from hand to hand. They were laughing, a noise which sounded out of place in the House of Gloom.

"Hey," Trent grunted at me when I entered through the back door.

"Hey." I was still keyed up from the Lucy situation and wasn't in the mood to socialize.

So, Aaron was going on with his life. He had the right

idea. We would all miss Lony, but tears couldn't bring her back. Sleeping fifteen hours a day only put off the inevitable. We all had to move on. Faint gray shadows were still visible beneath my brother's blue eyes and his smile still held a fake, plastic-like quality, but it was a smile nonetheless. He was trying.

Up in my bedroom, I decided I would try, too. I put the morning's events out of my mind and went to work catching up on my studies. If I was going to go back to school Monday, I needed to work hard to catch up to the rest of my class. Good thing it was still so early in the school year. I hadn't missed too many important tests or project deadlines.

I was in the middle of typing a writing assignment when my cell phone rang. I rubbed my eyes, strained from staring at a computer screen in the fading evening light. I flipped on my desk lamp and checked the caller ID. Bronwyn.

"So my parents wanted me to ask you . . ." she said, her tone dripping with reluctance, "The topic for Youth Group this week is *Placing Your Sorrow on Jesus,* like about dealing with grief when you lose a loved one, and they want me to invite you to come. There will be a guest speaker from Grace Christian who'll be talking about the loss of his daughter from cancer and then a group discussion."

"I don't know, Bron," I sighed and tried my best to be polite. "You know how I am about the religious stuff. And I'm not sure I want to work on my grief issues in a room with a bunch of kids I don't know."

"Oh, you are already going to a support group meeting up at the hospital? Too bad they meet on the same night."

*Ah, I get it.* One or both of her parents were standing over her making her call me. This kind of thing happened a couple of times a year, usually to invite me to a Youth Group social function or to a church service they thought might be of particular interest to me. Her parents felt it was the duty of all true Christians to "shepherd non-believers into the loving arms of the Lord" or some crap like that. As if for every person you converted you got bonus points on God's Great Scoreboard. I don't know, maybe they would win some prize when they got to heaven like a golden harp or a cloud with a view of the Grand Canyon. Being such a good friend, I decided to mess with her.

"Sure, Bron, I'd love to attend! I'll wear my leather teddy and carry a riding crop. Think a studded dog collar would be too much?"

There was a slight pause before she replied, "It's okay if you break down and cry. That's what support groups are for. I'm sure no one will fault you for getting snot all over your sleeve." I heard a murmured hiss in the background telling her to be more sensitive. I laughed.

"They say emotional trauma can cause teens to act out in inappropriate ways, but I would have given the football team blow jobs anyway. After all, they did beat Davenport last week."

Bronwyn made a choking sound like she swallowed a laugh and quickly covered it with a fake cough. "Well, okay, Cady, I'll talk to you tomorrow then. Bye."

I hung up the phone, my grin fading. I missed my best friend. The few times I saw her since the accident, her discomfort had been obvious. Bronwyn was great listener, but not so great at knowing what to say in awkward situations. I guess talking to me qualified as awkward now.

I opened a new window on my screen, and signed into Facebook. I'd been avoiding social media since the accident because I didn't really want to read the outpouring of sympathy from my classmates on my Facebook wall. It's not that I didn't appreciate the thoughts, I just couldn't deal with it all yet. A couple of days after the accident I posted a short thank you, and hadn't looked at it since. I wondered what the protocol was for deleting Lony's page. I could probably do it myself. She had never been very creative with passwords, and I'm sure I'd be able to hack it inside of five minutes, but was that right? Maybe Facebook has some sort of death cancellation policy where my parents could call them to delete the account.

Once Facebook loaded, I clicked over to Bronwyn's wall and left a message for her to meet me after she got off school tomorrow. It was time for me to start getting out of the house more.

That night as I was changing into my pj's for bed, Bryan phoned. Three nights in a row? He asked me about my day, and without planning to, I began telling him the story of Lucy and the mass in her lung.

"Are you sure you didn't feel a lump or something? Maybe something small enough that the doctor didn't notice?"

"I'm sure," I insisted. "It wasn't a lump at all. It was a vibration. And cold. You know, way cooler than the other skin around it. I thought I could hear it, too, but now I'm not so sure that part wasn't my imagination."

"Hmmm . . ." he pondered. "Maybe the mass inside the dog isn't a tumor at all, but an object. It might be radiating something, or you might have felt a magnetic pull. Were you wearing any metallic jewelry on your hands?"

"No. I didn't have jewelry on at all. Not even earrings."

"And the vet is going to let you know what she finds?"

"Yeah. Dr. Kristy promised to call right after the surgery. I thought about going out there, but I have my appointment in the afternoon."

"Ah, the therapist . . . You sure you don't need a ride?"

"I'm sure," I said with a smile. "Bryan, you don't have to be so nice to me just because my sister died. I mean, I appreciate your help and concern. You're about the only person I can really talk to right now, but I don't want you to go out of your way because you think you have to take care of me."

"Do you really think I'm just being nice to you because your sister died?"

The way he said it made me feel badly for even bringing it up. "I guess not. But . . . well . . . why are you being so nice to me? There are a lot of other kids in the school that you could be friends with who would be much better company than I am right now."

"I don't want other company. I want *your* company."

My breath caught in my chest and my brain froze for a comeback.

"I'll have my cell with me all day tomorrow," he continued. "If you want to get a hold of me during school, just text, all right? I'll talk to you soon. Sweet dreams."

I held the phone to my chest long after the line disconnected.

# Chapter 12

B Y THE TIME Dr. Kristy phoned at noon the next day, I'd caught my school work up in three subjects and was feeling pretty good. Hearing the doctor's voice —a mixture of intelligence and bedside kindness, which she used even when having the most mundane of conversations —brought back my concern for the little dog.

"How is she? How's Lucy?" I asked, my voice cracking a bit.

"Lucy's going to be just fine. She's still groggy from the anesthesia, and she'll have to wear an e-collar on her neck for the next couple of weeks, but she should be up and running around in no time."

"What was it?"

"Well, there was a mass on her right lung. I was able to remove it completely. I'll have to wait for the pathology to be completed before we'll know if it was malignant or benign, but I have high hopes. Lucy is only three years old, so even if it's cancer and we have to do chemo, she has a very good chance at a normal life."

A bit of the weight resting on my shoulders lifted.

"Cady," Dr. Kristy's tone turned hesitant, "I still would like to know how you were able to feel the tumor. Mark and I are going to do some research on it. I hope you don't mind."

"Not at all. I'm curious too. Nothing like that has ever happened to me before."

"Good. I'll let you know what we come up with."

After hanging up the phone, I showered and got ready for my appointment. What did one wear to see a psychologist? Would the doctor form opinions about me based on my clothing choices? You know, some sort of fashion Rorschach test? I wished I knew what kind of clothes crazy people wore so I could avoid them. I decided to go as safe as possible — dark jeans, an olive-green sweater and my hair slicked back into a ponytail.

When I finished, I walked quietly down the hallway to my mother's bedroom. If she wanted to go with me to my appointment, she'd have to start getting ready. I rapped at the door softly.

"Mom?" I called. There was no answer. "Mom, are you coming to my appointment with me?"

"Wha . . . ?" she said groggily.

I opened the door and stepped inside. "Mom, if you want to come with me to the grief therapist —" I couldn't finish my thought. Sadness dropped on me like an iron anvil falling on Wile E. Coyote in the old Looney Tunes cartoons. My palms went clammy and my pulse jumped. My heart broke in my chest all over again. I rubbed my eyes to keep the tears from spouting.

With great effort, my mother propped herself up on the edge of the bed. Her hair was a nest of tangles, greasy from lack of washing. On her night stand were several prescription bottles and an empty bottle of Gray Goose vodka. *Not. Good.* The room stunk of neglect and depression. What was it about this room that sent me into an emotional spiral? I'd felt fine two minutes ago. Now, I couldn't get my hands to stop shaking.

"Cady, hun, can you run a bath for me?" my mom asked. She was bent at the waist with her elbows propped on her knees. She rubbed her eyes with her fists so hard I worried for her corneas.

Steeling my shoulders, I pushed through the gloom. I didn't have time today for a breakdown. Forcing one reluctant foot in front of the other, I made my way to the bathroom. I plugged the tub and turned on the hot water, dumping a heaping dose of bubble bath into the swirling water, sending the scent of cucumber and melon swirling around the room with the steam.

I sat down on the closed toilet lid. The gloom was less intense in here, but no less depressing. Dirty pajamas and underwear were balled up in a heap behind the door. The towels were soiled and spots of water dotted on the mirror. These things just didn't happen in my mother's house.

Crossing over to the linen closet, I found a set of fresh towels and replaced the ones on the rack. I then scooped up the dirty laundry and piled it in the hamper, squishing it all in to fit. When we were expecting company or planning for an occasion, my mother occasionally would hire a maid to come in to clean. She received a discount because she referred the maid service to her clients for their open houses. I made a mental note to look up the woman's name in Mom's planner and have her come in, at least until Mom was back to functioning like a normal adult.

I blew my nose on a wad of toilet paper and took a couple of deep breaths.

"Mom," I said, leaving the bathroom. "I'll make some sandwiches for lunch. You should eat something. You look like you've lost twenty pounds."

She stood in front of her dresser, fingering a pair of socks like she couldn't figure out what they were for.

"Do you need any help?" I offered.

She looked up at me as if seeing me for the first time. Lately, that was how she always looked at me. "Oh . . . no. I'll be down soon."

"Don't forget the bath water. It's still running, and you don't want it to overflow."

She nodded, selected a pair of socks and closed the drawer.

By the time I reached the kitchen, my sadness had begun to abate. Maybe it was just the horror of my mother's depression that was triggering it. She was supposed to be seeing a therapist as well. She'd gone to two appointments so far, one while I was still in the hospital. Obviously, it wasn't working.

I slapped together a couple of double-decker PB&J's and set them on the table with an open bag of potato chips. I was almost done eating by the time Mom stumbled down the steps dressed semi-normally in wrinkled slacks and a sweater which fit her fine a few weeks ago, but hung on her now. Her breasts had shrunk so much, they were practically invisible under the fabric.

Just being in her presence filled my mind with grief. The strange thing was I'd thought I was getting better . . . or at least making some progress. I no longer slept all day, I was dressing in regular clothes rather than lounging in pajamas, I even went for stretches of time without thinking about Lony, not that she was ever very far from my thoughts. But seeing Mom set something off in me, triggering the sorrow to bubble back up.

I got up to wash the dishes so I didn't have to watch her nibbling at her sandwich with squirrel bites. We didn't talk.

I ended up driving us to the appointment in her BMW. She never mentioned that she was too impaired by pills to drive. She simply handed me the keys and climbed in the passenger side without a word.

We pulled into the parking lot of a new office building on the west side of town. My father's company had constructed the building only a year before. As with many of the buildings and homes he'd built, I couldn't look at it without pride catching in my throat.

Speaking of my dad . . . across the parking lot, he leaned against his work truck, talking to someone through his bluetooth. I didn't know he was coming, but the pleasure at seeing him improved my melancholy. Mom didn't have quite the same reaction.

"Julia," my father greeted with a bob of the head. He'd been calling the house every night to check in with Aaron and me, but Mom refused to speak to him.

With her lips pursed tightly, Mom wound her arm around my shoulders possessively and said, "Tim. We didn't expect to see you here. Do you have an appointment also?"

"Well, no, Julia, I'm here to support our daughter."

I hated this tension. It was so thick I was suffocating.

"Let's just go inside," I suggested, stalking off and not caring if they followed or not. I was so sick of the fighting. You'd think they could be a little kinder to each other in light of their daughter's death, but instead, the accident seemed to sever any lingering ties there might have been between them.

We entered the waiting room. Mom notified the receptionist we were here, then settled into a chair and roughly flipped through the pages of an outdated issue of *Glamour*.

Dad blew out a long breath of air and took the seat opposite her. He glanced at the magazines on the coffee table, but didn't see anything of interest. I gave him a weak smile which he returned just as weakly.

"Arcadia Day?" a woman called from the doorway leading back to the doctor's offices. All three of us stood and followed her down the hall where she invited us to sit on a couch in a comfortable looking office with purple walls and a stack of toys on the floor in the corner.

"It's nice to meet you, Arcadia. I'm Dr. Carrick, but you may call me Elaine. I like to keep things informal in this room. I find it helps us to get to know each other."

Elaine had one of those unfortunate faces with a weak chin overshadowed by a large overbite. Her nose pointed long and straight like a beak. Her eyes were soft and gentle though, the kind that might belong to a priest or grandmother in some movie where things were stereotypical and perfect.

"It's Cady," I said. "Arcadia is also too formal."

Elaine smiled and talked to my parents for a few minutes about what the goals were for my treatment and what they wanted me to get out of it. When that was done, she excused them to wait for me back in the other room.

The soft click of the door closing behind them brought back my nervousness. Sitting in a room with a shrink makes a person self-conscious. I stopped picking at my cuticles and folded my hands in my lap.

"So, Cady," she began. "Why don't you tell me about

how you've been since your sister's death. I understand you were in the hospital also."

Elaine was very easy to talk to, but I wasn't sure how much I trusted her. I started telling her about how each person in the family was dealing, omitting the part about my mother's drug stupors. I told her about my attempt to go back to school, but glossed over the details as to why I felt I had to leave after one class. Before I knew it, the hour passed, and I left with an appointment for the next week.

As we were leaving, Dad asked if I wanted to have a late lunch with him. I knew I shouldn't let my mom drive herself home, and besides, I had plans to meet with Bronwyn. The glint in his eyes dimmed when I asked for a rain check, making me feel both guilty and sad at the same time. He gave me a tight hug before climbing into his truck and driving away.

Mother was quiet in the car on the way home. Elaine had stressed during our session the importance of maintaining an open dialog with people to prevent feeling alone in my grief. I figured that was Mom's problem. She hadn't been dialoging with anyone except Prince Valium. Since I had her captive, I decided to confront her.

"Mom, I'm worried about you."

I felt her stiffen in the seat beside me, but she didn't say anything in response.

"I was thinking that until you're feeling better, maybe we could have that maid come in a couple times a week. I know how an ordered house always makes you happy."

Mom stared out the window a long moment before answering.

"Happy," she whispered as if it were a new vocabulary word that she was trying out on her tongue for the first time.

"Well?" I asked.

She sighed, "I guess."

Silence again.

"So," I said, grasping for something to say that might draw her out of her shell. "Aaron went back to school this week, and I'm going to go back on Monday. I'm almost caught up on the assignments that I missed."

Saying nothing, Mom pulled her sunglasses out of her Coach bag and shoved them on her face —the universal sign that a person does not wish to converse. Whatever. I focused back on the road.

"Swing in there, will you?" She gestured suddenly toward the Hy-Vee grocery store.

I braked hard in order to make the quick turn. The car was barely in park before Mom snapped open her seatbelt and flung the door open, narrowly missing hitting the side mirror on the Jeep parked beside us.

"Wait," I said, flipping the ignition off. "I'll go with you."

"Stay here," Mom snapped, closing the door hard behind her.

I watched her walk across the lot to the door, her gait slightly off. A few minutes later, she returned with a brown sack. The bag clinked as Mom slipped into the passenger seat and set it between her feet on the floor. I leaned over to peer into the top and saw at least four large bottles of alcohol and a small bag from the store's pharmacy.

"Let's go," Mom said, clicking her belt back into place.

I started the car and drove home, gritting my teeth the whole way.

The last thing my mother needed was more drugs and alcohol. Even if her doctor didn't know she was mixing, what kind of doctor prescribed that much medication to a woman who had nothing physically wrong with her? I mean, yes, her daughter died. It sucked. But it's not like if she slept long enough the sadness would magically disappear. My grip tightened on the steering wheel.

As we rounded past the high school, a thought occurred to me. Was it possible Mom was using more than one doctor to prescribe all of these drugs? There had to have been four orange pill bottles on her night stand this morning and a few more on the bathroom counter. As far as I knew, she hadn't been on any medication prior to the accident. That was a lot of bottles to accumulate in only a couple weeks.

Multiple doctors required the use of multiple pharmacies, right? Otherwise, the pharmacist would notice a person was being over-prescribed. I thought about this a moment. When I'd had bronchitis last year, Mom filled my antibiotics at the drug store next to the hospital. I'm pretty sure that was where she sent Lony to get her birth control pills too. I remember because she and Lony had gotten into an epic argument in the pharmacy parking lot while I sat captive in the backseat. Lony kept complaining that she didn't want to take pills that would make her fat when she and Cane weren't even having sex, but Mom had insisted on taking precautions. Yes, it was definitely the other store, not the one in Hy-Vee.

My skin paled as I began to realize my mother's problem was bigger than I'd thought.

# Chapter 13

I KNEW I should tell Aaron and my dad about my sus-
picions of Mom's drug use, but that would have to wait.
Shortly after arriving home, Bronwyn picked me
up in her mother's minivan and we headed to Culver's. We
were both completely in love with their mashed potatoes.
She also ordered a burger, and I a grilled cheese sandwich.
We slid into the corner booth where she began filling me in
on school.

"I should probably warn you," Bronwyn said, stirring
her gravy into her potatoes. "The cheerleaders want to put
together some kind of tribute to Lony during the half-time
show of the Homecoming football game.

"I don't care. It's not like I'm going to go to the game.
Oh, crap! I can't believe I flipped out over a stupid locker
memorial. Everyone must think I'm insane," I moaned, leaning my head on my hands.

"It's okay, Cady. No one blames you for it. Honestly,
they stopped talking about it already. You've been replaced

in the gossip chain . . . Sarah Conlin got knocked up by Chad Buss."

"For real?" I exclaimed. Sarah Conlin was the most popular girl in the sophomore class and the mayor's daughter. Chad Buss was a goofy looking senior with only a double-digit IQ.

"Yeah, they're neighbors, and I guess they've been fooling around in secret for a while. Now that she can't hide the evidence, Chad's been bragging about it all over the school."

"God, I can't imagine being pregnant at fifteen! I sort of feel sorry for her, but seriously, who doesn't know about condoms these days?"

"My parents probably think I don't," she said with a chuckle.

I grinned.

"So . . . how are you feeling?" Bronwyn asked.

I held a spoon heaping with potatoes and gravy in front of me, turned it over and watch the contents plop back into the cardboard container.

"I don't know. I mean, sometimes it seems to be getting a little easier, but then something will remind me of Lony and it all comes back. My mother is a completely different person. I can't be near her without getting completely bummed out."

She nodded and sipped from her Dr. Pepper.

"I've been trying to get out of the house a little more. Actually . . . there's this new kid at school . . . Bryan Sullivan? I met him right before Lony died. Anyway, he's sort of been helping me a lot."

My friend's eyebrows shot up in surprise. "What do you mean by helping?"

I filled her in about Bryan's brother passing away and

how he'd started calling me. I even told her about him being there for me the morning I tried to come back to school.

"So, do you like him? I mean, like a boyfriend?"

I blushed deeply and played in the mashed potatoes with my spoon. "I don't know. He's really a good guy. Cute. Seems smart. Plays guitar which is totally cool. But, I don't know, it's just not a good time for me right now to think about boys like that."

She agreed. "I bet it's nice to have someone to talk to who's been through it."

"Yeah . . . Oh, hey! You didn't work at the shelter yesterday did you?"

"No. I'm not scheduled until Saturday morning. Why?"

I told her about finding the tumor in Lucy's chest. I figured she'd hear about it from Gina or someone eventually.

"Weird," she said, with a hint of skepticism creeping into her voice. "There has to be an explanation for it."

"I know, but I don't know what it could be. Maybe Dr. Kristy will figure something out."

We finished our food and dumped the garbage in the trash can. We had time to kill before she had to go to church, so we stopped by the music store in the mall. As I was thumbing through the rack of t-shirts, I found one with two cartoon guys paddling a canoe down a river. The caption above the first guy's head read, "Paddle faster. I hear banjos." I bought one for Bryan, getting the guy behind the counter to help me guess the right size.

After leaving the store, I began to worry that Bryan would find my buying him a gift weird. I almost turned back to return it, but I decided to hold on to it and give it to him only if the right time came. If I chickened out, I could always give it to Aaron for Christmas.

Bronwyn dropped me on the curb outside my house. The evening air took on an autumn chill as night descended. My house was dark and foreboding. I checked the time on my cell phone. Only 6:20. The thought of spending the long evening in the House of Horrors made my stomach sick. I mentally ticked through my options then flicked out my cell phone to call my dad.

"Hi, honey," Dad greeted when he picked up. "What's up?"

"Um . . . I was wondering if I could come by and see your place."

"Sure! Come on over. Want me to order some Chinese for us?"

I wasn't that hungry since I'd eaten at Culvers only a couple hours earlier, but Dad sounded so happy by my visit, I told him to order me a couple veggie eggrolls.

When I hung up, I went straight to my car parked across the street, without stopping in the house first.

I parked behind my father's truck in front of the brick eight-plex apartment building. My parents own a few different rental properties around town. Mom would find deals on investment property and Dad would fix the places up, so they could sell them for a profit. When the real estate market tanked a couple of years ago, they decided to hold onto the places they owned and rent them out, rather than take a loss on the sales. They purchased this particular building the summer after I finished eighth grade. My dad paid us kids to paint all eight apartments and hallways. I didn't get that smell off of my hands all summer.

I rang the bell, and Dad buzzed me in.

"I'll get you a key made next time I go to Menards,"

Dad said as he opened the door for me.

I stepped inside and glanced around. "Still living in boxes?"

Cardboard U-Haul boxes stood stacked like skyscrapers around the apartment creating a skyline effect in the living room. The only thing that appeared to be put away was his extensive DVD collection which consisted of every John Wayne, Clint Eastwood and Al Pacino movie ever made.

Dad grinned guiltily, running his hand through his thinning hair. "Guess I just haven't had time to deal with unpacking yet."

I shrugged off my jean jacket and hung it on the back of a kitchen chair. I recognized the oak dining set from my Grandma Nora's house before she moved to Arizona a few years ago. When she left Iowa for a tiny condo in Scottsdale, she'd put most of the furniture from her large family-sized home into storage.

"Food will be here any minute," Dad said. "Have a seat."

I followed him over to the couch where I snuggled in and put my feet up. The comfortable sectional was also a relic from my Grandma's home. It was strange to think that my dad lived here in this place. It was all just . . . too bare. All of the walls were off-white and the carpets beige. Hotel rooms have more personality than this place.

"So . . ." I said, feeling rather awkward and knowing he did, too, "maybe after we eat, we could get to work on fixing this place up."

Dad nodded. "I was thinking, you know, if you want, we could fix up one of the bedrooms for you. It would probably have to be the small one, because Aaron may be moving in and if he does, he'll want the bigger room. You know, living here full time."

I nodded. "Aaron told me he wanted to move with you. Has he talked to Mom about it yet?"

Dad shook his head, "Don't think so." After a pause he added, "How is Mom anyway? She looked pretty rough today." This trial separation was something they both wanted, but the tone of his voice made it clear he was still genuinely concerned about her.

I debated about what to say. If I told him the truth, that Mom was turning into a junkie hermit, would that be disloyal to her? But what if protecting her was actually a bad thing? I decided to just be honest.

"She almost never leaves her room, Dad. She drinks alcohol and takes pills and sleeps like fifteen hours a day." I didn't mention my suspicion about her using multiple doctors. I didn't want to accuse her without concrete proof. I'd wait until I had a chance to take a look at those pill bottles. The prescribing doctor's name should be on them.

Dad drew in a sharp breath, but he didn't really look all that surprised. "Yeah, Aaron mentioned she was taking things pretty hard. Maybe —"

His thought was cut off by the tinny ringing of the doorbell. The food arrived. Dad took care of paying the delivery boy and brought the bag with him into the living room. I grabbed us two cans of soda from the fridge while he divided out the white take-out boxes between us.

I opened mine and let the steam escape from my egg rolls. Dad ripped into a package of chop sticks and began attacking his shrimp with lobster sauce. I picked up one of the crispy rolls and took a bite.

"Aw, man," I cried as I dropped my egg roll back into the box and scrambled for the can of soda. My tongue juggled the chunk of egg roll around my mouth, trying to keep it from burning my tongue into a melted lump of flesh. The cold Pepsi washed through my mouth like heaven.

"Careful there," Dad warned too late.

I set the food carton down on the end table. "I'll just give that a minute."

Something was off in the room, but I couldn't put my finger on what it was. The temperature seemed normal, but cool breezes kept brushing my skin. The ceiling fan above me was off and none of the windows were open. Something else about the room was making me uneasy, worried. I pulled my sleeves down over my hands and crossed my arms in front of my middle.

"So," Dad said, concern clouding his expression, "about your mother . . . I know you're worried about her. I am too. Just because things aren't working out so well with us right now, doesn't mean that I don't love her. What I'm trying to say here is that if you want me to —I don't know —take some action, I will."

My eyes narrowed, not sure whether I liked the sound of that. "What do you mean?" I asked.

"Well," he said, setting his dinner down. "To be honest, my instincts are to give her some time and let her ride this out. Losing Lony . . . well, it's been hell for all of us. I'm doing the best I can here, and I'm sure your mother is to, but if you think you might be in any . . . I don't know . . . danger or something . . ."

"She's not dangerous to anyone but herself, Dad."

He nodded. He let out a relieved sigh, and with it, a breeze, slightly warmer than the room, touched my face.

"But I am worried about her," I continued. "She's mixing booze with those pills. That can't be good. She stays in her pajamas all day and ignores the calls on her cell phone."

Dad's relief was short lived. He reached his hand up to rub the back of his neck. The coolness to the breeze was back.

"Do you feel that? That breeze? Where is it coming from?"

Dad held his hand up to check the air. "I don't feel any breeze." He shook his head and continued, "Well, I don't think I can help your mother right now. She won't even talk to me. Nora can't do much to help in Scottsdale. Think I should go have a talk with her therapist?"

I shrugged. "I don't know. What about Aunt Tina? I know she's your sister, but she and Mom have always been close."

Dad nodded, contemplating that option. "We could try it. I'll give Tina a call tomorrow. Just to be safe, I'll call her doctor, too. He needs to know that she's mixing her meds with alcohol."

Part of me felt badly for telling on my mother. When I was a kid, I once got in trouble for telling a neighbor girl that Mom made Dad sleep on the couch after they had a particularly bad argument. Mom sat me down and lectured me on what happens in our house is no one else's business, and I was not to tell tales about my parents to the neighbors. I had to wonder if this rule now applied to my father now that he no longer lived with us. I picked up my egg roll, now sufficiently cooled off, and began nibbling away.

# Chapter 14

BY SUNDAY MORNING, I'd gotten almost all of my homework caught up. Late in the afternoon, Bryan called to see if I wanted to do something. He picked me up in his car and we drove down to the river. Following alongside the Mississippi is a flood wall with a path on top where people can ride their bikes or walk. The tree leaves on the Wisconsin side of the river were just beginning to turn color. Bryan bought us ice cream cones at a stand, butter pecan for him and cookie dough for me. We ate them while we strolled along the path.

"You're not scared to go back to school tomorrow, are you?"

I shook my head. "No, not really. It can't be any more of a disaster than Tuesday."

"School was hard on me after Jesse died, but I got through it, and so will you."

Ever since he told me about his brother and that he had the same disease, I'd been waiting for an opportunity to ask him some questions. "Bryan, can I ask you something? It's kind of personal, so if you don't want to talk about it, that's cool."

"Go ahead. Ask." He picked a stone up off of the cement and tossed it out into the river where it sunk with a splash.

"Well, I've been thinking about what you told me . . . that you have that blood disease, too. Are you like . . . worried or anything? Like what if it was you?"

"Yeah, I guess so," he answered, then paused to lick the dripping ice cream off the side of his cone. "I mean, I've thought about it my whole life. My mother was insanely over-protective of both of us, especially when we were little. She actually homeschooled us until seventh grade because she was afraid we'd get hurt at recess or play too roughly with the other kids. Sometimes, it was hard to forget we were different."

"Wow. So she finally let you go to regular school?"

"Jesse used to beg our parents to let him go to school with the other kids. When he was fourteen and I was twelve, they finally caved, but we weren't allowed to take gym class or do sports."

"Wish I could get out of gym class," I muttered.

He grinned. "I may not have had to go to gym, but gym teachers have always found other ways to torture me, like writing essays on basketball theory or the history of physical education. Did you know the Victorians used to think allowing women to play sports was inhumane due to their delicate constitutions?"

"I think it's inhumane to make us all change clothes in the same room."

Bryan chuckled. "So, to answer your question about whether I worry about death, the answer is yes . . . and no.

I've lived with the possibility of death for as long as I can remember. I guess I'm sort of used to it. I try to remember that with treatment and a lot of caution, I could live a fairly normal life. But I'd be lying if I said there weren't times — especially after Jesse died —where I didn't feel the weight of it, you know?"

Not knowing what else to say, the best I could come up with was, "Um . . . I'm sorry. I mean, sorry that you have to live with this. So, like the disease . . . it is treatable, right?"

"Yeah. I take medication every day which has clotting factors in it. If a bleed happens, that'll help, or at least buy time for me to get to the hospital."

We sat down on a bench and watched a group of ducks bobbing along the shoreline. "Do you have bleeds very often?"

He shrugged. "Well, as much as my mother would like to completely encase me in Nerf, it's impossible not to. Jesse and I were more careful with each other than most brothers, but we'd still fight. When I was six, he threw a Hot Wheels car at me and cut my forehead open. I was in the hospital for a week. I also had some joint bleeding when I hit my big growth spurt freshman year. Most people don't realize that your joints are prone to bleeds. I guess growing seven inches in a year put stress on my knees, because they would ache and bruise up. Eventually, the pain went away, but the doctor says I might develop arthritis in them someday."

"How old were you when you got this?"

"I was born with it, but didn't start developing the symptoms for a few years. My mom was pregnant with me when Jesse was diagnosed. They knew I'd probably have it, too, so they banked my cord blood and had me tested right away."

"How scary for your parents! It must suck to have this

happen to both of your kids."

"Yeah, I think my mom wanted more children, but they decided to stop after me. If she'd have had a girl, the baby would've been fine, but there's no way to guarantee."

I didn't say anything, just wound a lock of my hair around and around my index finger. I loved the idea of having a ton of kids someday, and thinking about what Bryan's mom must have gone through made me sad. We nibbled our cones in silence.

"Well, I guess we better go," Bryan said. "I have a chemistry assignment to finish tonight."

"Yeah, sure." I popped the last bite into my mouth and wiped my fingers on a paper napkin before stuffing it into my pocket.

On the way home, I snuck a couple of glances at Bryan as he drove. We'd gotten pretty close in the time since Lony's death. And those black glasses that he drove with did things to his dark eyes that made my insides squirm. It was probably wrong for me to choose this time to develop my first real crush. (I'm not counting the unrequited love I have for Orlando Bloom.) Was there an appropriate amount of time a person had to mourn before they were allowed to move forward with their life? My guilt felt like a lead helmet on my head . . . two sizes too small.

How would Lony have dealt with it if our situations were reversed? If I was the one who died, leaving her behind? She already had Cane, so it's not like she would've stopped dating him just because of me. She also had a talent for selective thinking, not spending too much time on topics which depress her. Lony would have gone back to school last week when Aaron did. She probably would've roped her friends into putting together a memorial for me at the school, rather than ripping one down.

So, maybe I shouldn't feel too badly about my feelings for Bryan. I couldn't help the timing . . . heck, if it hadn't been for Lony's death, he probably would have never reached out to me.

# Chapter 15

"YOU CAN DO this," I whispered to myself. "It's no big deal."

I walked purposefully up the front steps of the high school, holding my worn —and newly mended —backpack like a shield. Ice water pumped through my veins, my body's reaction to the dozens of eyes following me down the hall. I wasn't being paranoid. The quick glances away when I looked up were proof enough.

The funny thing was I wasn't nervous at all about going to school that morning. I was actually looking forward to getting back to a routine. But once I entered the crowd of students, my stomach tensed up into one big knot and my skin grew damp with cold sweat. In fact, it was the most curious case of nerves I've ever felt; a mixed up cornucopia of emotions . . . excitement, joy, anger, fear. The walls of the hallway seemed barely strong enough to contain it all.

As I rounded the corner, there was Bryan, leaning up against the wall by my first hour government class, his attention on the battered Dean Koontz novel in his hands. I slowed my gait, pleased to watch him without notice. My pulse quickened and almost made me forget about the rest of the crowd. The intense gaze of his dark brown eyes seemed as if it might set the book on fire. Absently, he teethed his lower lip, drawing my attention to its full redness. His thick hair stood up funny in the back and he'd neglected to fasten the bottom button on his shirt, but to me, he looked perfect.

*Jeez, Cady. Stop being so sappy.*

"Hey," I said as I walked up beside him, trying my best to portray nonchalance.

Bryan startled at my voice, but then broke out into a big toothy grin. "Hey."

A boy trying to get into his locker nudged me over so my arm brushed up against Bryan's. Bryan could have stepped over, putting space between us, but he didn't. I'm not sure what it was about being near him, but those crazy mixed-up emotions faded, giving way to a relaxing calm.

"Are you all set to give it another go?" he asked.

I nodded. "I'm ready. I think."

"Good."

There was a slight rosiness to his cheeks which brightened up his pale complexion. Not a blemish on him. I pretended to bite my thumb nail in order to hide the zit which had poked out on my chin during the night.

"Well, I better get inside," I said, even though it was the last thing I wanted to do.

Bryan touched his hand to my shoulder for one brief moment and replied, "Yeah, I have to go, too. I just wanted to make sure you were all right. My phone's on vibrate, so if you need anything, text me." His hand patted the pocket where his cell phone snuggled against his heart.

As he strode away, I felt that strange tangle of emotions flood back. I clenched my jaw and entered the classroom just as the final bell rang.

I gave a hesitant smile to a few of those offering sympathetic looks as I walked to my seat. A feeling of deja vu came over me. Like the week before, my nerves felt like violin strings wound too tightly. I missed my name during roll call and the girl behind me had to poke me in the shoulder. My body temperature rose and I bit down on the end of my pen until my teeth left jagged marks.

Mr. Steele popped in a video on voting during the civil rights era and shut out the lights. I used the cover of darkness to get a hold of myself. Examining my emotions more closely, I realized that it wasn't all nervousness I felt, but a whole tornado of feelings at once —some of which didn't even make sense. There was frustration with my parents, anxiety over some big test which I wasn't prepared for, the triumph of first love. None of these emotions felt like they belonged to me, yet there they were, taking up residence in my mind.

I squeezed my eyes shut. The air in the classroom was thick with invisible smoke which clawed at my throat. I wanted to jump out of my seat and leave, but I couldn't risk another outburst like the previous week. Instead, I took some deep yoga breaths and tried to get a handle on myself.

When the video ended, Mr. Steele began asking questions to stimulate a discussion. I watched the final ten minutes tick off the clock and prayed he wouldn't call on me. He didn't. When the bell rang, I was out the door and halfway down the hall before most kids had a chance to gather up their books.

My next few classes were repeats of government. During third period gym, Coach Davis pulled me aside to talk about cross country. I hadn't run in weeks, and honestly, I hadn't given any thought to the meets I'd missed. Coach suggested that I withdraw for the rest of the season. I just nodded and wandered back to our dodgeball game. I knew I should be more upset about it. I loved running. But I couldn't muster up the energy to care about things like after school sports.

By the time I entered the cafeteria and sought out my usual table with Bronwyn and Shawn, my belly was all knotted up and I was wiped out.

My friends looked at me strangely when I sat down.

"Not eating today?" Shawn asked.

I shook my head no. "Not hungry."

Bronwyn's eyes crinkled with concern. "How are you holding up?"

I gave a one-shoulder shrug. How could I explain the weird feelings I was having when I didn't understand them myself? "Okay, I guess."

Shawn popped open a can of Pepsi and sucked the foam off the top with a slurp.

"Are you feeling okay?" Bronwyn prodded with concern. "You look kind of pale."

I waved my hand in the air like she was making a big deal out of nothing and plastered a fake grin on my lips which I hoped was passable. "I'm fine. Just feeling a bit out of the loop. Why don't you fill me in on what's been going on around here?"

Shawn took the hint before Bronwyn did and began to tell me about how he'd been cast as Sky Masterson in the fall musical, *Guys and Dolls*. I wasn't surprised he'd gotten the lead. Shawn had a baritone singing voice that could cause the hair to rise on your arms, and he was a natural comedian on stage. I focused on his crazy story about something that had happened in rehearsal, and that quieted the flurry of emotions in my gut somewhat.

A throat cleared behind me and a light touch fell on my shoulder. I spun around to see Bryan holding his lunch tray. "Mind if I join you?" The uneasiness on his face looked as if he were expecting me to say no.

"Of course not." I scooted over to make room for him on the bench beside me, but it was a tight fit between us and a group of sophomores sharing the long table.

Shawn jutted his hand out and introduced himself and Bronwyn. She flashed me a knowing look and a grin which caused heat to wash over my face.

"I've heard so much about you," Bronwyn said. "Cady was telling me what a big help you have been for her these last couple of weeks."

Bryan's eyes lit up at the compliment, and I didn't know whether or not to be embarrassed to have been caught talking about him. The denim of his black jeans rested lightly against my thigh, and it was all I could do not to press closer against him. The strange emotions rolling through me began to be replaced with a calm happiness.

"Bryan just moved here from Oregon," I said, trying to make conversation. This led to a discussion on how lame Dubuque must be after living in a big city like Portland. To our surprise, Bryan claimed to like it here.

"Don't get me wrong," he explained. "Portland is great and there is always lots to do, but I'm starting to get used to being in a city where I can get from one end to the other in less than a half hour and without ending up in a traffic jam. Before moving here, I thought it was going to be all cows and country music."

My friends and I groaned with the Iowa stereotype.

"But it's not like that here at all."

Shawn raised his right hand in oath, "I swear I have *never* milked a cow in my life."

Bronwyn giggled. "That's because you're scared of them!"

"Hey," he protested. "Those things are huge compared with a ten-year-old!"

"We went to a farm for a field trip in fourth grade, and Shawn literally squealed when a cow walked up behind him," she explained.

"It had this evil look in its eye," Shawn claimed. "I think it had mad cow disease or rabies or something."

"Oh, the Mad Rabid Cow of Iowa!" I exclaimed laughing. "Stop talking about it, or you'll scare Bryan away." It had been so long since I really laughed, and it felt wonderful.

Out of the corner of my eye, I noticed someone looking in my direction. Cane Matthews stood a few tables over holding his tray of food in one hand and a bottle of Vitamin water in the other. His glare turned my blood to ice water, halting my giggles instantly.

Shawn followed my gaze. "What's his problem?" he asked.

I shrugged and stared down at the table.

Bryan's gaze narrowed in on Cane, and he leaned a little bit closer to me.

"It must be hard on him to see Cady," Bronwyn answered. "She's like a living reminder of Lony."

"So? It's not like she can help it," Shawn stuck up for me.

I hadn't really thought about how it must be for Cane to face me, the mirror image of his dead girlfriend. A shiver rolled down my spine. I wondered how he was holding up.

Even though I always sort of thought of him as a meat-head, he always treated my sister well. He also had been the person standing closest to Lony when the train struck, which meant he'd had a front row view of the carnage, something I missed out on witnessing by passing out. Part of me wanted to go talk to him, to comfort him in some way, but I knew it would probably just make things worse.

After lunch, Bryan and I walked together to class.

"I like your friends," he commented. "They're cool."

"Thanks."

"So are Shawn and Bronwyn like . . . together?" he asked.

I couldn't help but chuckle. "No. Shawn . . . well . . . let's just say you're more his type than we are."

"Oh . . . I get it."

I glanced over to see his expression. If Bryan turned out to be some sort of homophobe, I might have to give this friendship another thought.

He just winked at me. "Shawn's cute and all, but I'm afraid my interests lean in another direction."

I blushed and then scolded myself. *He was not flirting with you! He was just letting you know he's straight.*

In lit class, the whirlwind of emotions crept up again, but Bryan's presence behind me helped me to keep them at bay. Focusing my mind on him distracted me from the other feelings. I even raised my hand to answer for the first time all day. But when lit was over, and I went to French class, I felt like a ship lost at sea.

I struggled to concentrate. Along with the variety of emotions I'd been experiencing all day, there was something darker coming over me, a deep black cloud of depression, different from what I'd been feeling at home. The classroom was set up with the desks in a circle to promote conversation. I peered around at the other students to see if they felt anything amiss. Some seemed tired, a few bored, and one guy bobbed his head up and down slightly to the beat of the ear buds under the hood of his sweatshirt. Around me, the flowery language filled the air like the scent of perfume at a funeral.

# Chapter 16

WHEN THE FINAL bell rang, signaling my release from school, I ran out the double-doors as fast as I could, my head spinning from the storm of emotions. The air was warm for late September, and my feet crunched the red and gold leaves under my feet. I didn't want to go home. Not yet. After the day I had, the last thing I wanted to do was return to the House of Perpetual Mourning. Rather than turning down my street, my feet trekked on aimlessly.

*What in the heck happened to me today?* It was something more than just sadness over my sister and the uneasiness of returning to school. It was like I'd been put in a clothes dryer filled with all of the emotions of everyone in the school and forced to tumble around with them for seven hours. I was worn out.

I turned down the next street over from my house. There was a small park a couple of blocks down where Bronwyn and I sometimes liked to hang out on the swings. A broken piece of sidewalk chalk was left abandoned on the ground, and I kicked it hard with the toe of my Sketchers.

"Cady!" a voice called to me.

I looked up from my feet and saw the strange neighbor woman, the one whose backyard met mine, grinning at me from her front stoop. How did she know my name? I lifted my hand tentatively and waved.

"Will you come here a moment? I'd like to speak with you," the woman said.

*Oh, no.* Was she planning on scolding me for spying on her with my binoculars? But she didn't look angry. Her expression was open and friendly. With a deep breath, I trudged up the walk to her front door.

"I have some lavender tea on the stove. Come in."

It's not like I was afraid of strangers, but this one made me uneasy. As if reading my thoughts, she assured me, "It's okay. I'm not some insane person who abducts children, I just want to talk to you about something."

Not wanting to admit that I *was* thinking she might be an insane person bent on abducting me, I followed her inside.

"My name's Jinx," she said. "Make yourself comfortable, while I get the tea."

Jinx disappeared into the kitchen.

The house was a Cape Cod, smaller than ours, and filled with . . . stuff. While I wouldn't exactly call her a hoarder, she obviously had issues with clutter. Books and newspapers were stacked in careless towers on the coffee table. Candles in mismatched holders sat on every available flat surface, including on top of an ancient console television and in the windowsills. A shaggy lapdog looked up from a doggy bed perched on top of a table next to the front window. He gave me a half-hearted "Arf" before resting his chin back on his paws and nodding off. I scooted a wad of blankets over and sat down on a red, crushed velvet couch that looked like it had time traveled here from the 1970's.

After a bit of rattling around in the kitchen, Jinx returned carrying two steaming mugs of light brown tea. I blew on mine and waited for her to say something.

"Honey?" she asked, squeezing a honey packet from KFC into her mug and stirring.

I shook my head no. I was really more of a coffee person, but I'd drink it to be polite.

"How do you know my name?" I asked.

She twirled her fingers in the air. "Oh, one hears things around . . ."

I nodded like I knew what she was talking about. I set my drink down on the coffee table to give it time to cool off, but then I didn't know what to do with my hands, so I picked it back up. My eyes wandered the room, unsure of where to look. I could sense the woman's gaze trained on my face.

"I'm very sorry about your sister," she said. Her expression was open and kind. Her large blue eyes were twin liquid pools. The wild cork-screws of her auburn hair gave her the look of a faerie tale creature. It was impossible not to like her.

"Uh, thanks . . ."

"How are you and your family holding up?"

I shrugged.

Jinx nodded.

"So what kind of name is Jinx?" I asked before I realized how rude it sounded. She didn't seem to take offense.

"Well, my real name is Jennifer . . ." She made a gagging motion with her finger to her mouth. " . . . but I got the nickname when I was a teenager and it stuck. Trouble used to follow me. Get it? Jinx?"

"Trouble used to follow you?"

"Oh, well, when you get older, life settles down naturally."

I lifted my drink and took a tentative sip. It burnt my tongue, so I set it back down. Not that I minded getting to know my neighbor, but I wished she would get to the point of why she called me here.

"So, you must be wondering why I asked you in," she said, tucking her bare feet up under her skirt so that she was sitting cross-legged in the recliner. The bottoms of her feet were dirty.

"Yeah, I guess I am."

"I need to tell you something that's going to sound crazy, but all I ask is that you don't leave until you've completely heard me out, all right?"

My belly fluttered. Should I be worried here?

"Don't worry," she said.

I began to wonder if my thoughts were being broadcast in a cartoon bubble over my head.

"Cady, I know what you are going through."

Oh, so that was it! Jinx must have had a sibling pass away or something and she wanted to comfort me like Bryan had. Made sense.

"So, did your sister die also?" I asked.

"Humph! Not hardly. She lives in Boca Raton and works as an investment banker. Not dead, but not much of a life either. No, I mean I know what is happening to *you* . . . emotionally."

"That's not hard to guess. My twin died. I feel like crap."

Jinx shook her head. I could tell she was going somewhere with this, but hesitated to explain it to me. "No, it's more than that. Tell me about school. How did you feel when you were around all of those other students?"

A flush spread across my face, and I darted my gaze out the window. I recalled the tornado of emotions. Could that be what she was referring to? If so, how did she know?

"Okay," she sighed. "Let go about this a bit differently. I have this . . . talent . . . I guess. Have you ever heard of telepathy?"

"Like communicating through minds?" I snorted skeptically.

"Yeah! See, I can read people's thoughts."

Terrified at the idea that what this woman was saying *might* be true, I tensed up, wrinkling my brow.

"Whoa!" Jinx laughed, touching her fingers to her temples. "You're a strong little thing! I can feel you trying to block me. I bet you don't even know you're doing it."

I shook my head in disbelief. "No, that's not possible. People can't read minds!"

"Oh, no? How is it that I know about the torment you went through this week at school?"

"It was my first day back, of course it was going to be tormenting!" I yelled without meaning to. I jumped up to my feet.

The little dog was startled by my sudden movement. He hopped down from the table and waddled over next to her chair like a guard dog. Yeah, the curly hair flopping in his eyes was terrifying.

"Wait, Cady," she said, reaching out to me. "Please sit. You promised to hear me out. I haven't even gotten to the part about you."

My knees locked in place. I didn't want to sit.

"Look, I appreciate you trying to cheer me up, but I really can't deal with crazy right now." I slid my arms into the shoulder straps on my bag and headed for the door.

Jinx shot to her feet, but didn't try to stop me from leaving. She just twisted her fingers together in frustration.

"Okay," she said, "leave if you want. But I want you to think about something."

I stopped in the doorway holding the screen door open, not turning around to face her.

"When your sister died, remember how you felt it? I mean really *felt* what was happening to her? Remember what you saw in that moment?" When I didn't answer she continued. "Come back to see me when you're ready to know what happened."

I walked out quickly, allowing the screen door to slam shut behind me.

# Chapter 17

THE RHYTHM OF my soles slapping the pavement in time to my breath had the power to relax me like nothing else. In the weeks since returning to school, I'd settled into a routine —school, work, jog, homework, bed.

The emotional storm of school wasn't abating. If anything, it seemed to be getting worse. Sitting in class felt like being tugged in ten different directions. Twice I'd had teachers keep me after class, their looks of pity only slightly hidden under concern. Of course, I couldn't tell them anything. I didn't know what was wrong with me. Mr. MacLeod, my physiology teacher even suggested I drop his class and try it again next year. I'd missed a ton of labs, and no matter how much I studied, I couldn't concentrate enough to memorize all of the Latin terms. I finally gave in and stopped by my guidance counselor's office to sign the drop forms. Of course it was too late for me to get into anything else, so I was assigned to a study hall for fifth period.

I rounded the corner of my street and slowed to a brisk walk. My breath sawed in and out of my chest through my mouth, and I used a cotton bandana tucked in the pocket of my jogging pants to wipe the sweat from my forehead. The autumn evening air caressed my damp skin, dotting my arms with goose bumps. From between the dwellings I could see Jinx's house, lights blazing in every room as if she had guests. For weeks I'd been telling myself that the woman was a fake, a charlatan looking to pull something over on the poor grieving girl. But then I'd find myself wondering about the possibility that she was telling the truth. Other than the little bit I mentioned to the doctor in the hospital, I hadn't told anyone about actually feeling Lony's death, about seeing it through her eyes. There had to be a logical explanation for how Jinx knew all this, but for the life of me, I couldn't figure out what it was.

So I did the only thing I could do —I took to the Internet. For weeks I'd read everything I could find on the subject of telepathy. At first, I only found websites advertising psychics and fortune tellers who would answer your questions for a price. My only experience with psychics happened at the Dubuque County Fair a couple summers ago when Lony talked me into getting my tarot cards read. All the woman told me was that I needed to work hard in school in order to get ahead in life. Duh! I could tell better fortunes than that. I can't remember Lony's fortune, but I'm sure it mentioned nothing about her early death.

After weeding through the fakes and weirdoes, I came across websites that included scientific studies and testimonials about telepathic experiences. To my surprise, a fair number of scientists believed communicating with the mind was real. There was even a doctor down at the University of

Iowa Hospital, Dr. Ulrika Helbo, who had done actual studies and written books on the subject. I spent part of an evening reading different papers and things that she had published in medical journals. She basically believed that humans were born with ten senses. In addition to the five physical senses of touch, sight, smell, hearing and taste, there are five senses of the soul —intuition, peace, foresight, trust, empathy. She claims telepathy is simply a manifestation of our sense of intuition.

In an article in *The New England Journal of Medicine*, Dr. Helbo sighted evidence that early humans used the power of the mind and energy to transmit information, much the same way our other senses work. But as humans evolved, they began relying more on the other five senses, allowing the others to go dormant, like an appendix or something. Interesting stuff, and she had a lot of documentation to back up her theories, but I was a believe-it-when-I-see-it kind of girl.

Standing on the sidewalk sweating, I gazed at Jinx's house and wondered if I should just give her a chance to explain. After a moment of staring, I decided to try a little experiment. I balled up the damp bandana and stuffed it back in my pocket. I walked around to my back yard where I took a seat on a wicker patio chair. I knitted my brow and concentrated on her kitchen door. *Jinx, can you hear me? This is Cady. I'm in the backyard. If you can hear me, I'm ready to talk.*

A moment passed.

And then another.

Maybe I was out of her range. *Or maybe she's just a fake.*

I was silently chastising myself for my stupidity when Jinx popped out her door, grinning so big even in the dimness I could see the full row of her teeth.

"Cady!" she called out waving. "Sorry, I was on the phone."

Shock pinned me to my spot, preventing me from answering. *She heard me. She really heard me!*

Jinx waited patiently by the fence separating our yards while I processed. After a minute, I got up and walked toward her.

"Believe me now?" she asked without a hint of I-told-you-so in her voice.

I lifted one shoulder in a shrug. "I don't know."

Jinx nodded. "Fair enough. Want to come over and talk?"

"Is now a good time? I mean, it looks like you have company or something."

She glanced back to her house to see what I was seeing. "Oh, no. I just have a bad habit of not turning lights off when I leave rooms. Not very *green*, I know!"

"Well, let me take a shower, then I'll be over."

Twenty minutes later, I was standing on my neighbor's stoop with wet hair and a hollow feeling in my stomach from skipping supper.

"Come in," Jinx said, with the door held open for me.

The living room was the same chaos of clutter that I'd seen before, but with the soft light emanating from the mismatched table lamps and a few candles, it was homier this time. The strong scent of sandalwood drifted up in wisps of smoke from an incense cone on the coffee table. From his bed, the dog lifted his head so he could peek at me from under his bangs.

"Can I get you something to drink?"

"No, thanks," I replied, sitting down on the edge of the

couch.

"Thank you for coming back," she said with an understanding smile, before taking a seat across from me.

I pressed my lips together. I didn't know how to start or even why I was there. I guess when people drop the bomb on you that they are psychic, it piques your curiosity.

"I'm not saying I believe you or anything," I started, "but you must have had a reason for telling me about your . . ." I couldn't say it. It was all too ridiculous.

"I know how this sounds to you," Jinx said with a sigh. "I always have this problem when I tell people I'm a telepath. Most think I'm a fake, that I must be secretly Googling them in order to act like I can read their thoughts. But honestly, this isn't a parlor trick. I wish I could escape it sometimes."

"Well, like I said, I'm not saying I buy into this, but I want to hear more. Can you like . . . talk to me without speaking?"

"No, the connection only works one way. I can hear thoughts of others, but I can't send messages back."

"Convenient," I replied. Her claim would be easy to prove if she could communicate something to me.

"No, actually it's not convenient. It's damn frustrating sometimes."

She obviously didn't pick up on my sarcasm.

"Why are you telling me this?" I asked.

Jinx unfolded her legs and leaned forward, focusing a serious gaze on me.

"I'm telling you this in order for you to understand how it is I know certain things about you."

A chill ran through me. "So you can hear my thoughts even when I'm all the way over at my house?"

"I have about a three block range. Give or take depending on how strong the person is broadcasting."

I pictured our neighborhood with its rows of houses. Three blocks in every direction would include not only houses, but a gas station, a Catholic church and the small strip mall on Asbury Road . . . even the high school athletic fields and parking lot.

"That's a lot of people."

She sighed and frowned. "I know. I can tune most of it out now, but the buzz is always there, like background noise. I have to actually pay attention to focus in on a particular voice. Some people transmit more clearly than others. Their emotional state also makes a difference. If a person is calm, their thoughts are quieter, but if they are upset or excited, the thoughts can be loud enough to wake me from a sound sleep."

"So when Lony died . . ."

She nodded. "Yeah. Your household practically has its own channel now. Your brother is the worst."

"Seriously? I would have thought that would be my mother."

"No. Your mother is sad and having a hard time, but her thoughts are muddled with intoxicants. She sleeps a lot, and I don't pick up on dreams too clearly. But your brother isn't sleeping much at all. He's really suffering deeply."

I never would've guessed. Aaron always acted so aloof.

"What about me? I assume that's what you wanted to talk to me about."

Jinx took a deep breath in and out as if buying time to weigh her words. "You are also suffering, obviously, but you're stronger than they are. You're pulling through it well. You're lucky that you have such nice friends to support you."

I didn't say anything. My mind ticked through the last

few weeks wondering what things this woman might have eavesdropped on. I still didn't really believe her. Psychics are fake, right? I decided to test her again to be sure. I plastered what I hoped would be a neutral expression on my face, relaxed, and then shouted with my thoughts, *Stand up!*

Jinx hopped to her feet, sending the little dog scurrying under the coffee table. "Like this?" she asked.

My jaw fell open. "Y-you heard me!"

She rolled her eyes. "Of course I did! You yelled at me! Can I sit again?"

I nodded.

"Any other experiments you want to try? Guess what number you're thinking or something?"

I shook my head no.

"Okay, then." She scooped the dog up and set him on her lap, threading her fingers through his tiny curls. "So, the reason I wanted to talk to you is because I noticed something going on with you that you are not aware of yet."

"If I'm not aware of it, how would you know? I can't be thinking of it." I was trying to sound like a smart ass, but the shakiness in my voice betrayed me.

"You're not thinking of it, but I recognize the signs and feel an obligation to tell you."

"Okay . . ."

"During your sister's accident, you know how you saw the whole thing through her eyes? How you felt like it had been happening to you?"

The blood drained from my face. I did not want to talk about this.

Jinx continued on. "And you know how when you go near your mother, you suddenly get depressed, even if a few minutes earlier you were just fine?"

I barely nodded. How could she know this stuff? There had to be another explanation.

"And at school, you feel a jumble of emotions . . . more than the usual teenage girl mood swings."

She was right. The things I'd been feeling in the past few weeks hadn't been normal. Maybe some of it could have been explained by Lony's death, but when I added it all together, something wasn't right.

"What's happening to me?" I whispered.

Jinx set the dog aside and knelt in front of me, folding my hands in both of hers. "You've heard that twins have psychic connections, right?"

"Yeah. Lony and I used to dream the same dreams sometimes when we were little . . ."

"And you have probably heard about auras before too, right? The psychic energy field that surrounds us? Some people can see them. I can't, but some can."

I nodded.

"Well, when your sister died, your auras connected . . . they reached out to each other. I've heard of it happening before. That's how you could feel what your sister experienced in those last moments."

I let that explanation sink in. The doctors at the hospital wondered how I was able to experience physical shock when I should have only felt an emotional one.

Jinx continued, "After the accident, your aura was stretched. It didn't go back to its normal shape around you."

"My aura is *broken*? What does that mean?"

"It means that whenever people enter your aura range, you can feel their emotions."

I considered all of the strange emotions I'd had that week. My mother made me depressed. Being around Bryan calmed me down. Being in a classroom filled with hormonal teenagers sent me in circles.

"So . . . so I'm psychic?"

"No, honey. You're an empath."

# Chapter 18

"EMPATH . . ." I whispered, feeling the word on my tongue.

Jinx hopped up and retrieved a book from her stuffed shelf. "Let me show you."

As she flipped to the table of contents and located the section she was searching for, I checked out the title of the book. *The Guide to Modern Psychic Phenomena* by C. C. Knight, PhD.

"Here we go," she said as she moved to the couch next to me, so I could follow along as she read aloud. "'An empath is someone who is sensitive to the psychic energy and vibrations of others. Because emotions are charged with life energy, the empath experiences the emotions as their own. When the emotions are positive, this can be beneficial to the receiver; however, when the emotions are negative, the receiver is in danger of depression, bouts of rage and exhaustion. Empaths have been known to turn to drugs or alcohol as coping mechanisms. Many admit to having thoughts of* *suicide.'"*

"What!" I interrupted. "I'm going to want to kill myself over this?"

Jinx shushed me and continued reading.

*"'The best way for an empath to combat these negative symptoms is by first, recognizing the difference between genuine emotions and those that are imposed on them, and secondly, by surrounding themselves with positive people. Some empaths claim to be able to block the emotional energy of others, and even convert negative energy into positive and channel it back to the sender, thus improving the emotional health of the sender . . . '"*

Jinx closed the book and gave me a pat on the knee. "Cady, I know a woman, Sophia Blackwell, who is also an empath. When I began noticing the symptoms in your thoughts, I called her for advice. She has learned how to develop and control her gift, and has given me some suggestions on how I might be able to help you do the same. Sophia would love to help you herself, but she is getting up there in age and lives out in Sedona, Arizona. Traveling here is not really an option for her now."

I didn't say anything for a long moment while I let it all sink in. It wasn't that I doubted the existence of psychic energy, in theory. What I had trouble with was the idea that *I* had any psychic ability. While I basically had a healthy self-image, I never really thought there was anything special about me. I had no other real talents: I was cute, but not beautiful; smart, but not a genius; well liked, but not popular. I was as middle of the road as a teen girl can be. Why would God or fate or the cosmos or whatever decide to give this ability to *me*?

"Are you okay?" Jinx asked.

I nodded. "I'm just absorbing."

"I understand. I went through the same thing when my telepathic gift started to manifest. I was thirteen at the time. At least you have someone like me to help you." Her mouth twisted into a troubled frown.

"Is that why you're being so nice to me? Because you went through it alone?"

"That's one of the reasons," she replied, setting the heavy book down on top of a pile of fashion magazines. "I also couldn't sit back and watch you deal with everyone else's grief on top of your own. That's way too much for one girl to handle."

I recalled my mother holed up in her bed and how crippling it was on me to go near her.

"What was it like for you? I mean when you started reading minds. Did you think you were going crazy?"

A shadow covered her eyes and I felt a slight ripple of emotion emanate off of her. Now that I knew the wave of sadness wasn't coming from me, I could almost track the source back to Jinx. It made me wonder if I would be able to trace emotions to specific people in crowds.

From the expression on her face, I figured her story must be difficult to think about. What felt like a cool breeze blowing from Jinx's direction tickled my arms, but when I looked down, the light hairs didn't so much as tremble. The wind wasn't physical. My belly tensed with a sadness that I didn't understand. After a long time, she began to speak in a voice, barely above a whisper.

"I didn't think I was crazy, but everyone else did. My mother passed away when I was only three . . . breast cancer . . . so I lived with my father and step-mother."

She tugged on the tight springs of her hair as she spoke.

"I figure it must have been puberty which brought my abilities out. That happens to some people. Sometimes, the opposite happens. A child will be psychically sensitive and then begin repressing it in puberty. Anyway, that's when I really began to notice it with me. It came on gradually. You know, I'd think someone said my name when no one did. I'd answer a question that hadn't been asked aloud. It really freaked people out. The kids at school started to distance themselves from me. My step-mother, who never cared for me to begin with, would complain to my father, saying he had to do something with me and that I gave her the creeps. When I tried to explain to them what I was experiencing, Millicent —that's my step-mother —convinced my father that I needed psychiatric care."

My stomach began to tighten with anger. This time I could sort of tell that it wasn't coming from me. Jinx closed her eyes for a moment. The ripples of frustration evaporated, replaced by a soft calm. She continued.

"I spent my high school years in and out of mental institutions." Her shoulders shook from an involuntary shudder. "I had to get a GED, because sitting in a classroom was too difficult for me. I wasn't as good at blocking thought feeds as I am now, and that made it hard to concentrate on the teachers."

Flashes of that emotional tornado from earlier popped into my head. Would I have to go through that every day until I graduated? What about college?

Jinx continued, "It was when I was staying in a group home in Oklahoma that I met another girl, Bridget, who also was a telepath and, like me, whose parents sent her away. The difference was Bridget's abilities were far more advanced than mine. She helped me by teaching me blocking techniques and how to focus on specific thought feeds. I don't know what I would have done without her."

"What happened to her . . . to Bridget?" I asked.

"She's married to an insurance agent and has three kids. They live in Atlanta or Macon or someplace like that. But in order for Bridget to live a normal life, she has almost completely given up her abilities. She's been blocking everything for so many years now she can't take the blocks off any more. Only rarely will a word or a phrase break through, and only from someone who is an extremely strong broadcaster."

I brightened. "That's great! You mean I can learn to block this out completely? You have to teach me! When do we get started?"

Jinx frowned and the crease between her brows deepened like a swollen river. "Cady, be careful to weigh all of your options before you decide to do something like that. Our abilities are gifts, and your gift is a part of you. Never be quick to give up a piece of yourself."

"Right," I said with a shrug. "I get to be the psychic equivalent of an emotional dumping ground and will probably end up as a suicidal alcoholic. Nope. The sooner I can block this stuff the better."

She didn't look very happy, but seemed resigned to let it go for now. Instead, she picked up one of those long candle lighters and began flicking it, watching the tiny licks of flame.

"So, what happened after you gained control over your abilities?" I asked. "Did your parents let you come home?"

"No," she replied with a sigh. "You see, my father is very . . . prominent. Back in the early eighties, he built a large technology company from the ground up and it was very successful. By the time I was eighteen, he and Millicent and their kids were like this big happy family where I just didn't fit anymore. Besides, Father was starting to get interested in politics. The last thing a politician needs is a crazy daughter running around ruining his image."

"So, what did you do then?"

Jinx inhaled deeply through her nose and let it out with a whoosh through her mouth blowing out the weak tongue of flame. She dropped the lighter back down on the end table. "Honestly? He bought me off."

"What do you mean?"

"My father set me up with a large trust fund under the condition that I disappear."

"Are you serious?"

She shrugged with one shoulder. "It's not like we were close anyway. He worked constantly when I was growing up, and I never saw him. Millicent couldn't stand me and didn't want me around her kids. I figured I would just go off and start my own life, so I moved to Dubuque. The end."

I thought about my own parents and what it would be like without them. Sure, things were strained in my family now, but no matter what happens I know they love me. Whether they would believe that I'm an empath or not is another story. My mother is intensely skeptical about all things that can't be proven scientifically. My father might be more receptive, but it's hard to say.

"So, you just, like, live off your trust fund? Or do you work?" I asked.

"I never touch that money if I don't have to," she said with a tone that implied that money was tainted. "I live off of my gifts. I'm a life consultant."

"A what?"

"A life consultant, a therapist. I got my degree in counseling through an online program and now I meet with people who are having problems and give them advice."

"Lots of people are therapists. Where does the whole using your gift thing come in?"

"I listen to the things they aren't telling me. It makes me much more effective than a normal therapist. Most people censor their words, only speaking in partial truths. I'm not saying people are dishonest, just selective. My gift enables me to serve them better."

I shook my head in wonder. Outside the window, I spotted a sliver of moon in the inky black sky, reminding me of the time.

"It's getting late. I better get home before my mom worries."

Jinx grinned. "She's sleeping. Wish I could read dreams better. I'm seeing flashes of a shirtless Hugh Jackman."

*Ew.*

I stood and stretched.

Jinx walked with me outside where she bent to retrieve a soggy Shopper Stopper from the ground next to her steps.

"When do we begin?" I asked. "With the whole blocking thing? If I'm going to make it through high school, I have to find a way to ignore my classmates."

"I don't have regular work hours. I work by appointment only, and I always go to my client's homes. If my car is in the driveway, I'm home." She inclined her head toward a newer model VW Beetle parked a few yards away. "Feel free to stop by when you have time."

I gave one last wave to Jinx before she turned to go back inside, and I headed home.

# Chapter 19

AFTER SCHOOL THE next day, I fumbled with the dead bolt lock on my front door. I was already inside, but couldn't get my key out. Lony and Aaron never had trouble with this lock, but for some reason, it just didn't like me.

The muffled sound of Florence + The Machine began playing on my cell phone in my backpack. I let the keys dangle and dug it out.

"Hello?" I answered, still concentrating on not breaking the key off in the door.

"Cady? It's Bryan. Is this a bad time?"

"No. I'm just getting home."

With a hard tug the key gave way, smashing my elbow against the wall.

"Son of a —!" I censored myself just in time. I held the phone in the crook of my neck so I could rub my funny bone. "Ouch!"

"Are you okay?" Bryan asked. "What happened?"

"I'm all right," I groaned. "No big deal."

"Uh . . . do you have plans for dinner? Like with your family, I mean?" he asked.

"No. My mother hasn't been up for cooking much lately. Why?"

"My parents are going out with one of my dad's new clients. I was wondering if you wanted to go get pizza or something."

*Whoa! Is he asking me on a date?* My spine tingled at the thought. But what if I was overreacting? What if this was just a friends thing? Best to play it cool.

"Um . . . sure. Sounds good."

"Pick you up around six?"

We hung up, and I barreled up to my room. It was too early to get ready, so I dug out some homework to work on. Concentrating during school was a nightmare, so I had started putting in extra effort into my assignments at home in order to make decent grades.

At school that day, I thought a lot about the whole empath thing and that storm of emotions that overcame me whenever I was around people. As much as I didn't want to believe it, Jinx was right. I was picking up on the feelings of others. For example, I used the bathroom pass during study hall, and when I entered there was a freshman girl splashing water on her face at the sink. She'd been crying and her mascara streaked down her cheeks like skid marks. I didn't mean to gawk at her, but the vibrations of anger rolling off of her and into me glued my feet to the spot. Goosebumps rose on my arms as the sinking feeling of betrayal coursed through me. I knew for sure these emotions were not coming from me. Two minutes earlier, I had been walking down the hallway humming along with a song stuck in my head.

When the crying girl noticed me, she glared at me through the mirror and stormed out in a huff, followed by her cloud of cold rage.

I shook my head to clear my thoughts. I really needed to put this empathy stuff aside for a while and get some school work done.

When my history assignment was finished, I stood and stretched. The emotional tornado was taking its toll on my muscles, filling me with tension. I yanked out the band holding my ponytail, brushed my hair out and slid a thin headband in to keep it out of my eyes. Other than some light lip gloss, I hadn't worn makeup to school. I wondered whether I should at least brush some mascara on or something. *Jeez, it's just pizza!* I scolded myself. *It's not like this is a date . . . is it?*

I left my jeans on, but traded my "Buffy staked Edward" t-shirt and hoodie for a light green peasant blouse. I surveyed myself in the mirror on the back of my bedroom door. Nice enough, but still casual. From my school bag, I took some cash out and tucked it into my jeans pocket. As much as Lony had tried to make me, I never took to carrying a real purse.

The doorbell rang. I rounded the corner at the top of the stairs, and to my horror, my mother was standing with the door open looking at Bryan shift his weight from foot to foot. Thankfully, she wasn't in her bathrobe, but a pair of yoga pants and a t-shirt. I cringed at the sight of her matted hair on the back of her head.

"Mom," I called out, hurrying down the stairs. "This is my friend, Bryan Sullivan . . . from school. Bryan, this is my mom."

My mother turned at my voice and looked at me funny, almost like she couldn't remember how she got there. "Oh . . ."

"We're going to go get some pizza. Do you want me to bring you anything back?"

She shook her head. "No, I'm not hungry." She started to trudge up the steps toward her bedroom, but as an afterthought she added, "Don't stay out late."

I watched my mother disappear around the corner with my jaw hanging open. *Are you kidding me?* Whether it was a real date or not, this was the first time a boy picked me up to take me out to dinner —other than Shawn anyway, and he didn't really count. I guess I'd have thought my mother might take a bit more interest. After all, Bryan could be a meth addict or a convicted felon for all she knew. When Lony first started seeing Cane, my parents insisted on getting to know him before they would let her go off with him alone. For two weeks, he had to endure awkward family dinners and watching TV with Lony in the den while my parents wandered in and out like an Army patrol to make sure they maintained clothes on and hands visible at all times. It's not that I wanted Bryan to have to suffer through an embarrassing third degree. I just thought she would have cared more, that's all.

"Ready?" Bryan asked, holding the door open for me. I could feel his nervous energy tingling my skin. I rubbed my arms briskly.

"Sure," I replied, brushing past him out the door. I smelled the light spicy scent of cologne and smiled. He normally didn't bother. I was glad I gave in and brushed on mascara.

"So," he asked, opening the car door for me. "Where is the best pizza in Dubuque?"

"Oh, easy. Happy Joe's."

"Happy Joe's it is then."

Bryan circled the vehicle and got in. When he twisted the key in the ignition music blasted out of the speakers and he fumbled to turn it down.

"Sorry," he said with an embarrassed grin. "I like it loud when I'm alone."

"No prob. I do the same thing," I replied. "What group is this?"

"It's my cousin's band, Crescendo. He's the drummer. They play small venues in the Portland and Seattle areas. This is their demo."

"Not bad," I said bobbing my head a bit with the beat.

I directed Bryan to the pizza place. We ordered my favorite, half taco/half BLT. Bryan cringed when I told him the BLT side used mayo in place of pizza sauce, but his attitude changed once he took a bite.

"I'm not a vegetarian exactly," I explained, plucking the sausage bits off of my slice, "I just don't really like meat very much. It's a taste thing more than a moral thing."

"So you don't eat steak?"

I shook my head. "Nope. I tried a bite of my dad's once, but didn't care for it."

"More for me, I guess." He reached for his second slice. "I'm not picky with food at all. My mother is the must-clean-your-plate type. I learned a long time ago that if I didn't want to end up having my dinner for breakfast the next morning, I better get it over with and eat it while it's fresh."

We chatted easily through dinner, but when Bryan got up to order us some ice cream sundaes, Jinx cropped back up into my mind. All through dinner I had been trying to pay attention to my emotions and the people around me, but

I couldn't tell if I was reading people right. In the car, Bryan had seemed nervous, but I wasn't picking any of that up from him now. In general, I was feeling happy and calm. How did I know that was my real feelings or if they were coming from someone else near me? What kind of range did this empathy thing have anyway?

Across the dining room, I spotted a toddler who was throwing some kind of tantrum. His face was red and he wailed at the top of his lungs. The young mother kept trying to shove ice cream in his mouth to shut him up, but all that did was cause melted ice cream drool to run down his chin and neck. It gave me an idea for an experiment.

I checked on Bryan and saw he was still waiting to place our order. I stood and started walking toward the little boy, going slowly enough that I could concentrate on any feelings I might be able to pick up from him, yet fast enough so that it would look like I was casually heading toward the restroom.

Twenty feet from the boy and I felt nothing.

At fifteen feet, I bent down to pretended to tie my shoe. The feelings of general happiness were faded, but I wasn't necessarily picking up on anything negative. I stood up and began walking forward again.

At ten feet, I stopped next to an empty table and picked up the menu lying on it. A stirring began in my belly that had nothing to do with the pizza I'd just ate. My face started to heat up and uneasiness crept over me. As I pretended to be checking the specials, I concentrated on the cool waves of feeling I was getting from the toddler's direction. There was anger and frustration . . . a little bit of discomfort too. Of course, the frustration could have been coming from the mother also, who was digging in her diaper bag for something to appease her child.

Just as I was setting the menu down to step closer, a freezing jolt shot through me as the boy lifted his fork and threw it as hard as he could onto the floor where it bounced and landed a few feet in front of me. A clear and distinct shock of rage ran through my body and settled somewhere deep inside me. I gasped audibly. The mother apologized as she came over to retrieve the fork, but I could only nod with my mouth hanging open dumbly.

*Oh. My. God. Jinx was right.* I guess up until that moment I hadn't fully believed her, but standing there with my head throbbing with a cold headache and my nerves on edge, I had to admit there was something weird going on. The little boy watched me with big brown eyes, his rosy cheeks tear stained and drool running from his lower lip. He didn't feel as upset anymore. I guess throwing the fork got whatever it was out of his system. The mother glanced up at me and flashed a wave of embarrassment mixed with confusion. I pivoted and returned to our table.

I buried my face on my hands, squeezing my eyes shut so hard I could see spots swimming in the blackness. *What does this mean? What am I supposed to do now?* I didn't want to go through life experiencing the emotions of everyone around me! How am I supposed to go into a crowded situation like a concert or a movie theater ever again without turning into a complete head-case? *Oh, no. How am I going to be able to handle school?* A groan escaped the back of my throat.

"You okay?" Bryan asked, a cool brush of concern touching my body.

I jerked my head up to see him setting our sundaes down on the table. "I'm fine," I said, managing a weak smile. "Just a bit of a headache."

His forehead wrinkled. "Do you want me to take you home?" The vibrations of his concern increased.

"No, I'll be okay." Forcing a fake smile, I dipped my spoon into the chocolate ice cream with warm peanut butter topping and took a small bite. "Ice cream cures headaches, you know. It's scientifically proven."

"Mmmm . . ." he replied, swallowing the cherry from the top of his banana split. "I always knew ice cream had to be good for me. What else can it do? Cure the common cold?" The coolness of his concern warmed into something more pleasant.

I nodded. "It's good for colds . . . the flu too. Also, sprained ankles, upset stomachs and gout."

"Gout?" he laughed. "In that case, I think I'll have my mother stock up our freezer with Rocky Road. I wouldn't want to come down with gout."

I watched Bryan as he talked and ate his sundae in large, enthusiastic bites. When he smiled I noticed one of his teeth was a bit crooked, overlapping the one next to it. It's funny how an imperfection like that can add so much character to someone's face. He had a bump on the top of his nose. And a tiny mole at the base of his throat bobbed up and down as he swallowed. The skin of his neck looked so soft. I wondered what it would be like to press my lips against it. My gaze lifted and I realized Bryan had stopped talking and was looking at me curiously. I was pretty sure my face was as red as a tomato.

"What are you staring at?" he asked. "Do I have hot fudge on my face or something?" He wiped his mouth with his napkin.

"No . . . I'm sorry." I shook my head, feeling like an idiot. I stirred my ice cream slowly to have something else to focus on.

"I don't mind, you know . . . you looking at me, I mean."

A shock of invisible electricity jumped between us, making my heart pound. I peered up from under my lashes to see him grinning at me. The heat in his eyes matched the warmth I was picking up from his soul, causing my palms to go damp.

"Whatever," I said dismissively, trying to play it off as a joke. "Are you almost done, because it's a school night, and I have to get home before you turn into a pumpkin."

"Well, in that case, we better go. Orange is not my color."

Bryan tossed a tip down on the table, and we headed out to his car. It took almost twenty minutes to get back to my house. While Bryan talked, I amused myself bathing in the warm caresses of his emotion. At first, I only felt a general feeling of contentment, kind of like a warming in the belly. It was the feeling that I got most often from him. He must be a naturally happy person, I concluded. But as we rounded the turn onto my street, I began to pick up on some anxiety vibrating off of him. I glanced over at Bryan, now who was grinning and telling me a story about something that happened at jazz band rehearsal, and wondered what he had to feel so anxious about. This emotion reading thing was interesting, but without knowing the reasons behind the feelings made it darn frustrating.

My house was mostly dark when we pulled up. A faint glow of light from the basement windows indicated Aaron was holed up in his room. I could also see the violet flickering of a television on in my mother's bedroom. She hadn't even left the porch light on for me.

Bryan trailed behind me up to my front door, his hands

shoved deep down in the pockets of his jeans, his shoulders rounded. I fumbled to fit the key into the door lock in the darkness. Stinking dead bolt!

"Here, let me help," he said.

I handed him my keys and stepped out of the way. With a jiggle and a flick of his wrist, the bolt shot open.

"There you go." He picked up my hand, placed the keys into my palm and closed my fingers around them. But he didn't let go. At his touch, I felt his nervousness amplified.

We stood there for a moment, both of us looking at my small fist cradled in between his two large hands, his thumb rubbing my skin in lazy circles. His palms were soft but the fingers on his left hand and right thumb had calluses. I ran my finger over the thick pads.

"From playing my guitar," he explained, the tone of his voice thick.

"Do they hurt?" I asked softly. We were standing close enough that I could feel the warmth rising from his skin.

"Not anymore."

He reached for my other hand, folding it into his. "Your hands are so cold," he commented.

*That's because all of my blood has risen to my face.* "And you're so warm."

But it wasn't just the warmth of his hands that were heating me up. Waves of excitement and anticipation rolled between us. My heart palpitated wildly.

I raised my eyes to meet his. Though the corner of his mouth curved upward, his expression was serious. Even in the dark, I could see his gaze dip to my lips.

Bryan lifted a hand to touch a lock of my hair. So softly I could barely hear it, he whispered, "Cady, I want to kiss you."

Somehow I was able to swallow the lump in my throat and reply, "I want you to kiss me too."

A glimmer of exhilaration flashed in his eyes as he leaned down and slanted his lips on top of mine. It wasn't the first time I'd been kissed —I guess I had to count Tyler Galvin from ninth grade —but being able to feel the emotion from both mine and Bryan's perspectives was almost indescribable. Waves of nervousness turned into waves of pleasure as our lips parted deepening the kiss. The soft scent of his cologne mingled with the sweetness of his ice cream taste, making my head swim with delicious intoxication.

My breath became ragged as adrenaline coursed through our bodies. I gripped his shoulders for fear my legs would melt out from under me. Bryan placed a warm hand on the small of my back and threaded the fingers of his other hand through the back of my hair, sending shivers down my neck. Energy flowed back and forth between us in each place we touched like feedback. So complete was the emotional circuit between us, I almost couldn't sense where I stopped and he started. I pushed my body against his, unable to get close enough. The pressure building and building until —.

Bryan's mouth lifted from mine. I gasped. I could still feel the humming between us, but there was also a twinge of disappointment . . . on both of our parts, I think.

He touched his forehead to mine, his eyes drifting closed. "I wish I could stay here and kiss you all night, but my parents are probably home and wondering where I am."

With reluctance, I took a shaky step back. "See you tomorrow?"

"Definitely." He gave my hands a final squeeze before turning to walk back to his car. I waited until he pulled away from the curb before going into the house.

I ran up the stairs and flung myself on top of my bed. I could still taste him on my lips, smell him on my skin. I replayed the kiss over and over through my mind. Man, that boy could kiss!

I rolled onto my side, curling around a pillow. So, what did it mean? I now knew for sure that Bryan liked me, but how is it I really felt about him? Did I want a boyfriend? I kind of liked not being one of those girls who spent their entire high school years obsessing over some boy. It just seemed too exhausting. But Bryan was different, wasn't he? When I was with him, things felt easier somehow. His calming presence soothed the stress of my life.

A short vibration in my pocket alerted me to a text message. I reached for my phone and checked the screen. The message was from Bryan and it read, "THAT WAS FREAKING AMAZING!"

*Yes, it was.*

# Chapter 20

I TOOK MY car to school the next day, so I could go straight to the animal shelter after classes ended. When I pulled in, I spotted Shawn leaning against his car, fiddling with his iPhone. Only he could pull off plaid pants and make them look stylish.

"Die, Pigs!" he grunted through clenched teeth as I approached.

"Playing Angry Birds again?" I asked.

He glanced up at me and gave me a half smile before turning his attention back to his game. "Yeah . . . it's addictive."

"Well, put it away. The bell is going to ring in like three minutes."

"Fine," he grumbled, locking his phone and shoving it into his back pants pocket. "I called you last night, but you didn't answer your cell."

"Yeah," I said, as we walked toward the building, "The ringer set on vibrate, so by the time I noticed you called I was getting ready for bed. Did you need anything important?"

"Not really . . . just wanted to ask you about Bryan."

"What about him?" I asked, trying to project casual disinterest while my insides turned to spaghetti at the mention of his name.

"Well, yesterday at lunch . . . he looked kinda into you."

"Did he?" I asked, unable to keep the grin off my face.

Shawn laughed and shucked my arm. "Aw, man! You do have the hots for him!"

"Shut up," I replied, giving him a little shove.

"Well, you do right?"

"I guess . . ."

"Cady's got a boyfriend . . ." he teased, but only loud enough for me to hear. "Seriously, I think it's cool that you're finally interested in someone around here. He seems like a cool guy. Those eyes are to die for."

"I know, right? His lips are even better."

"Girl, you've been holding out on me! You have to call me tonight and tell me everything."

Inside the doors, Shawn and I headed our separate ways with promises to see each other at lunch.

I floated through the hall with a smile on my face. It was crazy how good I felt for someone who had tossed and turned the whole night before. The memory of that fiery kiss and the emotions that came with it played on a continuous loop through my mind all night long. It was the best I'd felt in weeks, and I didn't want to let it go.

I was so caught up in my thoughts, it wasn't until Mr. Steele was well into his lecture that I began to notice emotions in the classroom besides mine. They seemed to swirl around me in a steady hum. If my range really was about ten feet, I figured over half of the students and Mr. Steele would fall within it. I struggled to keep my body relaxed and mind open. The only way to get a handle over this empathy thing was to understand it.

My eyes drifted closed so I could concentrate on identifying the different emotions around me. A sluggish feeling seemed to dominate. Tiredness? That would make sense given that it was first hour. It could also be boredom. There was a wave of excitement coming from somewhere . . . behind me? Yes, I could sense the direction. I snuck a glance over my shoulder and saw Sarah Dobbs staring at the clock, her fingers drumming the cover of her textbook. Yes, the excitement was definitely coming from her.

My thoughts were interrupted by Mr. Steele passing something out, and I realized with horror that we were having a quiz. *Crap!* I might be back to school physically and making an effort to keep up on my homework, but I hadn't been paying much attention in class.

My panic must have shown on my face, because when Mr. Steele set the paper down on my desk he said, "Just try your best."

A ball of worry sat in my stomach, this time I was fairly sure it was my own and not my classmates doing it to me.

When I flipped the quiz over, I scanned the questions. The whole thing was short answer. *Oh, come on! No multiple choice?* At least then I would've been able to guess at the answers. I groaned loud enough that the boy in front of me, Ben . . . something, turned and looked at me. I glared at him and read the first question to myself.

What are the three branches of the U.S. government? Well, that one was easy. I wrote, "Judicial, Executive & Legislative." Maybe this test wouldn't be so hard after all.

How many years make up a term for Senators? I didn't

know. I jotted down four years, since I know that's how long Presidents are elected for.

How many members make up the House of Representatives? *I don't flippin' know!* I left it blank.

By the time the bell rang and students began piling their completed quizzes on the corner of Mr. Steele's desk on their way out, over half of my page was still blank. Oh, well. I slapped the paper on the desk and hurried out of the classroom. I was so lost in my own thoughts I almost ran into Bryan, who was waiting for me outside the door.

"Whoa, there!" he said laughing. "You looked like you've been chewing on glass. What's up?"

"We had a quiz, and I'm fairly sure I bombed." We strolled down the hall toward my locker. "I just don't get what's happening with me and school. I mean I used to study really hard and get good grades, but now," I sighed, "I just don't care anymore."

Bryan nodded and put his arm out to keep me from getting jostled by two boys who were play-fighting in front of us. "You're probably still feeling lost from missing so much school. Have your parents talked to your teachers about how you're going to deal with the work you've missed?"

"I don't think our parents have even noticed that Aaron and I have gone back to school yet. Besides, I caught up on my missed work. It's the problems of concentrating in class that is getting to me."

When we got to my locker, I spun the combination and switched out my books. There were still bits of tape stuck to Lony's from where I'd ripped the pictures down. I closed the metal door and glanced up at Bryan, leaning next to me with a lazy grin on his face. All of my tension melted away.

Bryan reached out and picked up a lock of my hair,

twisting it between his fingers. "You have the softest hair I've ever felt."

"Um . . ." I wanted to compliment him back, but wasn't sure what to say. *Gee, I really think you're hot*, just didn't seem right. " . . . thanks."

There was a strange expression on his face . . . like he wanted to tell me something, but couldn't get the words out. I concentrated on the emotion vibes he was sending out. It was tough to isolate him in the sea of students around us, but when I took his hand in mine, it was like all of the conflicting waves cut off and I was perfectly in tune with him. Touching him seemed to block out the feelings of the students around us, so that his emotions commanded my full attention. What didn't make sense was the strange tension I was picking up from him.

"Is something wrong?" I asked.

His eyes widened as if startled out of some deep thought. "Uh, I need to talk to you about something."

"Okay." *Oh, no! He regrets kissing me!* "What is it?"

He glanced around at the thinning crowd. "Not now. We have to get to class. Want to go get some coffee or something after school?"

"Sure." I didn't know if I could wait that long. "Just tell me this one thing or I'll obsess over it all day . . . are you going to tell me that kissing me was a mistake?"

One side of his mouth curled up into a grin. "Are you kidding? Kissing you was the most fun I've had all year." To prove it, he leaned down and gave me a soft, lingering peck on the mouth, sending my pulse into a stampede. "I just have to explain something to you. It's not that big of a deal, really."

"Okay. I won't worry about it then. See you at lunch?"

"Yeah," he replied, giving my hand a squeeze before dropping it.

We headed off in different directions, me walking on clouds the whole way to second period, my botched quiz long forgotten.

As I stood at the cafeteria salad bar trying to decide between limp romaine and limp spinach, Bronwyn approached with a playful glare on her face.

"So," she said, "when were you going to tell me you and Bryan are dating? I'm your best friend, and I had to hear it from the gossip chain?"

"We're not dating . . . exactly. That is . . . I don't know what you call it." I decided on limp spinach, but drowned it in ranch dressing.

"But the two of you were making out against your locker today?"

My head snapped up in surprise. "We weren't making out! We barely kissed!"

She chuckled at my reaction.

"I can't believe you even heard about that. Dang. I don't know why the school invests in an intercom system when all they have to do is send the morning announcements out through the grapevine."

She laughed and the florescent lights glinted off of her retainer wire. "So it's true? That's so cool! How long has this been going on?"

At that moment, I honestly don't think anything could have wiped the smile off my face. "Oh, Bronwyn! He's so incredible!" As we stood in line at the check-out, I filled her in. "We had our first official date last night, but you know we've been talking for a few weeks now. And when he dropped me off, he gave me this good-night kiss that was so hot, it practically peeled the paint off the front door."

Bronwyn stared off dreamily. "Sounds wonderful!"

"It was! But you know, I'm not exactly sure what this means. I mean, it's not like he asked me to be his girlfriend or anything. I just don't know where it stands right now."

"But you are going to go out with him again, right?"

"That will be $4.15," the lunch lady sporting a hair helmet said as she weighed my salad. I handed over exact change, and we made our way to our usual table in the back.

"Of course, I'll go out with him again. In fact, he asked me to have coffee with him after school today. It will have to be fast though. I'm working at the shelter this afternoon."

When we got to our table, Shawn was already there with Angelique Rasmusson, a senior girl who hangs out with him once in a while. I don't know her all that well, but she's in the drama club with Shawn.

"Hi, Ang," I said as we sat down. I made sure to keep the spot next to me open for Bryan. "What's up?"

"Bonjour," she replied. Angelique has this whole French thing going on. She dresses like Audrey Hepburn and smokes unfiltered cigarettes. "Colin and I broke up, so Shawn agreed to stand in as my Homecoming date. We're trying to figure out what to wear. I want to do a whole 1940's theme. What do you think?"

"Oh, that's this weekend?" A little knot formed in my gut. If Lony had been alive, she would've been talking about the dance non-stop.

"Yeah," Angelique replied. "It's kinda last minute, so we have to hit the stores after school today. There's this really chic vintage place down in the Cable Car Square that I want to check out."

With a model perfect body like Angelique's —rail thin

with legs that went on for miles —she could wear a trash bag and make it look like something off the cover of Vogue. "I'm sure you'll find something."

A warm hand touched my shoulder. I looked up to see Bryan beaming at me. He set his tray down next to mine. On it was a plate with a pile of overcooked spaghetti.

"Hey," he said in a general greeting to the table as he slid in next to me. Shawn flashed me a knowing grin and my cheeks pinkened.

"Hi, Bryan," Bronwyn replied. She quickly introduced him to Angelique.

Angelique tucked a lock of her short dark bob behind her ear, drawing attention to her long graceful neck and gave him a smile that managed both flirty and pouty at the same time. "Hello," she said, "I don't think I've seen you around here before. I would have remembered."

I ground my teeth together. Do guys really go for such obvious flirts? Yes, actually, they do.

Not Bryan though. As he said, "Nice to meet you," he gave my shoulder a light squeeze, giving the not so subtle hint that he was already taken. I warmed at the brief touch. Angelique's stupid grin faded and she turned her attention back to Shawn.

"So, are you going to be able to get your dad's car, or will I have to drive us?" she asked Shawn.

"I'll ask," he replied gulping a big swig of milk from the carton. "I've had my license for a month already and he's still afraid to let me drive."

I don't think I blamed Mr. Cole for not wanting Shawn to go off alone in his Lexus. Let's just say that Shawn passing his driving test must be proof of divine intervention.

A couple of senior girls called out Angelique's name

and waved her over. "I have to run. Meet me by my locker after seventh period," she said to Shawn before rushing off.

"So you're taking Angelique to Homecoming?" Bronwyn asked. "What happened to Carlos?"

Carlos Espinoza was a really cute senior that Shawn had been "talking to" for a while.

Shawn rolled his eyes. "Who knows? One minute he acts interested and the next he avoids me like the flu."

"He's a jerk," I said.

Shawn sighs. "No. No, he really isn't. It's just that he's closeted with his family still. How they can't tell is beyond me! That queen can set off gaydar alarms ten blocks away."

"Sometimes parents don't really want to see their kids for who they really are," Bryan said, twirling his fork to roll the long noodles up into a bite-sized nest.

"I know mine don't," Bronwyn agreed. "My parents still think I'm ten years old."

I smirked, remembering the dollhouse Bronwyn received for her fifteenth birthday. The miniature hand-carved furniture pieces were cool and everything, but what was she supposed to do, play with it? It'd been taking up a whole corner of her bedroom ever since.

"So," Shawn said, obviously wanting to change the subject, "you two are going to Homecoming, right? If my dad won't let me have the car, maybe we can double together."

A shot of fear hit my chest like a bolt, and I realized it was coming from Bryan, whose knee was resting against mine. I glanced up to see him biting his lip and looking pale. What was the big deal? Why didn't he just tell Shawn that he hadn't had a chance to ask me? It's not like I wanted to go anyway. I'd rather have him come over to watch a DVD or something.

"Um . . . well . . ." Bryan hedged. "*I'm* going . . . but not with Cady."

I felt like the bench I was sitting on dropped out from under me, sending me into free fall. A pained look crossed his face as he tried to explain to me, but his words made no sense. Girlfriend? Flying in from Portland? Planned months ago?

My belly roiled and the smell of the ranch dressing was making me want to hurl. I mumbled an excuse and left the table, dropping my lunch —tray and all —into the garbage can.

I burst through the bathroom door, nearly hitting some girl in my rush to get to a stall where I locked myself in and sat down hard on the seat. *What in the hell just happened?* I asked myself, hot tears dripping onto my lap. *How could I be so stupid?* Here I thought Bryan was this great guy, but really he'd been playing me. *He has a girlfriend back in Portland? Don't you think he could have told me that before ramming his tongue down my throat?* I sobbed silently, feeling my life slide back down into the shit-pile it had been ever since my sister died. Maybe this was karma's way of biting me back for trying to be happy before my sister was even cold in the ground.

When I heard Bronwyn come in asking if anyone had seen me, I tucked my feet up out of sight until she left. Girls came and went from the bathroom through the rest of the lunch hour. I knew there was a line waiting to use the toilets —I could sense their impatience —but I refused to vacate my stall. The bell rang indicating the end of lunch. Five minutes later it rang again signaling the start of sixth period. I was alone at last.

I wadded up a bunch of toilet paper and wiped at my

face. I dropped it in the bowl and flushed. As I left the stall, I met my gaze in the mirror, cringing at the sight of my red-blotchy face under the harsh florescent lights. No way was I going back to class.

Leaving the bathroom, I walked to my locker to get my backpack from where I'd stashed it before lunch. On my way out of the school, I passed Ms. Schilton, my freshman English teacher. She opened her mouth as if to ask for my hall-pass, but something in my expression must have warned her to back off.

When I got in my car, I turned the ignition and let the engine idle. Where would I go? It was too early to go to the shelter. I didn't have to be there until four. No way was I going home. A note from my mother left on the kitchen table this morning told me that the cleaning lady was coming in, and I should gather up my laundry. The last thing I wanted was to have my pity party interrupted by some stranger vacuuming my bedroom.

I put the car in gear and drove out of the lot. Without really thinking about it, I found myself pulling up in front of Jinx's house. As I walked up her sidewalk, she opened the door for me.

"Must've heard me coming, huh?" I said with a forced, humorless laugh.

"Oh, honey, what happened?"

I flopped down on her couch, not bothering to move the newspaper that was left there. The dog yipped and cuddled next to my feet. I wanted to tell her, but my mouth refused to form the words.

"Oh, no!" Jinx exclaimed sitting down beside me. "He has a girlfriend?"

"Well, that's one benefit of having a friend who can read

minds," I muttered. I reached down to pet the dog. He snuggled in closer, laying on top of my sneaker now.

"That makes no sense. You should have heard his thoughts last night. He was so into you! And that kiss . . ."

"You eavesdropped on our kiss?" I stared at her wide-eyed.

Jinx fiddled with clasping and unclasping her charm bracelet. "Well, it was hard not to. You two broadcasted your thoughts so loudly."

I wanted to be mad at her for invading my privacy, but who was I to judge? I'm sure people wouldn't like knowing that I could read their emotions either.

"So, are you going to tell me what he was thinking about?" I asked.

Jinx shook her head. "No way. I learned a long time ago to keep the details of people's thoughts to myself. Let's just say he wasn't thinking about anyone but you."

I wanted to press her, but I understood she was trying to respect Bryan's privacy. What would it matter anyway? He has a girlfriend, so it's not like I have any future with him now.

"What's your dog's name?" I asked as a way to change the subject.

"Pavlov."

"Nice." I scooped Pavlov up and hugged him to my chest. He wiggled and wagged so excitedly you'd think he'd just won the lottery. "He's a Pomeranian, right?"

"Pom-Poo . . . half Pomeranian, half Poodle. So how was school today? I don't mean the Bryan stuff . . . I mean the empathy."

I set the dog down and watched it trot off toward his leopard print doggie bed. "It's still really annoying, but I think I'm starting to understand it a bit more."

I filled her in about my experiment at the pizza parlor. "I figure my range is about ten feet. I also notice that the sensations are more intense if I'm touching a person."

Jinx nodded. "That happens with me too. When I make direct contact, it's like tuning a radio and all of a sudden you hit the perfect frequency. That one message is so strong that it blocks out the messages from everyone else around me."

From the pocket of my jean jacket Florence Welch sung out. I fished my mobile out and checked the caller ID. It was Bryan. Lit class just got out. My finger hit the button to silence the ringer without answering.

"Not going to talk to him?" Jinx asked, a wrinkle of disapproval forming between her brows.

"No, he can wait. I just don't want to think about him right now."

She sighed. "Okay, then, how much time do you have? We could work on teaching you how to create blocks to keep emotions out if you want."

"Sure, I have two hours before I have to be at work," I replied.

"I'll go get us some sodas and then we'll get started," she said patting my knee as she bounced off to the kitchen.

A short vibration buzzed from my phone, indicating a text message. I peeked at the screen.

"WE NEED TO TALK."

I ignored it. I knew on some level that I was acting childish. It's not like he'd been my boyfriend or anything. He could go to the stupid dance with anyone he wanted. It's just that I really thought he liked me. Now, I had to wonder whether he was just being nice to me because Lony died and he felt sorry for me.

"IF YOU DON'T ANSWER, I'M GONNA HAVE TO TXT THE WHOLE STORY TO YOU & WILL TAKE ALL DAY . . ."

I jabbed the off button hard. Let him text until his thumbs bleed. Didn't mean I had to read it.

Jinx returned with two Diet Pepsis, set the drinks on top of a stack of mail strewn across the top of the coffee table and dragged a chair up so that she sat across from me, our knees a foot apart.

"Okay . . . so learning how to block signals takes practice. You might get a bit of a headache at first, but like any other muscle, once you get used to using your mind in this way, it'll get stronger and it won't bother you anymore."

I nodded.

"Now, tell me what you are sensing from me right now."

I studied the woman in front of me, sitting cross legged. I wasn't getting much of anything off of her. Dressed in a pair of ancient Levi's and an apple green t-shirt, her springy hair tangled up into a bun held in place by a couple of wooden pencils, Jinx appeared to be totally at ease.

"I don't feel much from you. Just a general feeling of contentment," I said.

She grinned, "Good! I've been feeling very even-keel today —not too happy, but not upset or anything either. Now, I'm going to think about something that will change my mood. Let me know what you feel."

She lowered her gaze to her lap, but her face remained perfectly neutral. I wondered again how old she was. Her oval-shaped face was un-lined, but her eyes held wisdom in their depths, giving her an ageless feel.

After a moment, the atmosphere in the room changed. Low levels of vibration tickled my mind. I tasted them with my sixth sense.

"There's something . . . not quite sadness . . . more like nostalgia. Longing?"

Jinx giggled and the vibrations changed to a warm happiness. "That's so cool! I was thinking about my mother. She died when I was so young that it's hard to feel sad about it. I just sort of miss her, you know? I always wondered what it would be like if she had lived. Let's try another one!"

She steadied her face again and concentrated. This time the buzzing grew with tension. My pulse increased a little.

"Anger?" I asked. "Frustration?"

"Yep," she said, letting the emotion fade. "My cell phone company completely screwed up my bill this month and I spent half of the morning yesterday on the phone with —" she raised her fingers in air quotes " —customer service, which was really just a call center in Bangalore or someplace."

I was pretty pleased with myself. Maybe this empathy thing wouldn't be so bad when I got used to it. I picked up my soda and took a long swig, letting the effervescence tingle the inside of my mouth before swallowing.

"All right," Jinx continued, "I'm going to summon that same feeling again, only I want you to try to block me."

"How?" I asked.

She pursed her lips together and squinted. "I don't know. That is, I don't know how to describe it. It's second nature to me now. Okay . . . use your mind to feel the signal that I'm broadcasting." She must have turned her thoughts back on Bangalore because the frustration meter ramped up again. "Can you feel it?"

"Yes," I replied. My eyes drifted closed. Slowly, I reached the tendrils of my mind out to touch the emotions between us. I felt around them, stroking the edges, letting them lap at me like waves rolling and retreating on the wet sand of a beach.

"Now," she whispered, trying not to break my concentration. "Block me."

I flexed my mind, squeezing my fists tightly. The sand on my inner beach began to rise, holding the waves back. I could still feel the vibrations out there, but they couldn't quite reach me. The muscles in my abdomen and shoulders flexed to lend my mind additional strength, but after about thirty seconds, I lost my grip and Jinx's frustration came pouring through.

"Stop!" I shouted a little louder than I'd meant to.

Jinx let her thoughts fade back to neutral. "That's good . . . really good! You actually had me blocked there for a while. How do you feel?"

The "little headache" that she'd warned me about was actually an ice pick being pounded into my frontal lobe. I rubbed my temples in slow circles.

"Ah, your head hurts. Told you that would happen. Want me to get you an Ibuprophen?"

I shook my head. "No, I'll be okay. Let's do it again."

# Chapter 21

AS I PULLED into the parking lot outside the shelter, my brain trembled with a full blown migraine. I accepted some pain reliever from Jinx before leaving her house, and she assured me that the ache would go away soon, but I wished I could go home and crawl into bed. I was ready for this day to end.

Bronwyn's car was parked in the lot, too. The mortification I felt at lunch seeped back. *God, how could I have let Bryan lead me on like that?* I chastised myself silently for not asking him about his girlfriend status when we first started talking.

Maybe, I'd get lucky and Bronwyn wouldn't bring it up.

"Hi, Cady," Gina said as I walked in the front door. She had her school books splayed out in front of her on the front desk. She worked at the shelter as a vet tech while in veterinary school.

"I can watch the desk for you," I offered, knowing that it was Gina's least favorite job.

"Nah," she replied, biting on the end of her pen. "It's been really slow today, so I don't have much else to do. Dr. Kristy is doing paperwork and Bronwyn was waiting for you to come so you guys can walk the dogs together."

I nodded. "Okay."

I stopped by the break room to stash my backpack before heading out to the kennels. At the sound of the door hinges, the dogs went nuts, barking and wagging their tails to get attention. Bronwyn was refilling water dishes that had been drained or tipped over during the day.

"Hey," I said.

"Oh, hi," she replied, the compassionate look on her face echoed the soft waves of worry coming from her. "How are you? I tried calling."

"Oh, yeah. My phone's off."

Her brows crinkled together in reproof. "So you haven't talked to Bryan then?"

I sighed. "No, and I'm not going to either."

"Cady —"

"Save it, Bron," I snapped a little louder than I'd intended. I felt a twinge of hurt flash off Bronwyn, but it was gone just as quickly. "I don't want to talk about it anymore."

She sighed and rolled her eyes to the heavens. "Okay, fine. But I want the record to reflect that I think you should hear him out."

"Noted."

I walked over to the leash cabinet and began untangling a few that had fallen to the bottom. By the time Bronwyn finished with the water bowls, I had six dogs leashed up and ready to go.

"So," she said, as the dogs tugged us along in their excitement. "You haven't told me how school is going for you since you've been back."

What could I say? While not as fanatic as her parents, Bronwyn's faith in religion was pretty strong. She wouldn't even read the horoscopes in the newspaper because she believed they were demonic. How would she react to the revelation that I could feel her emotions vibrating off of her whenever she stepped within my aura field? Would she think I'm possessed or something?

I just shrugged. "It's okay, I guess. No, actually, it sucks, but I can feel it getting better."

"Understandable," she replied. A lab mix that I didn't know spotted a squirrel and yanked hard on her arm. "Patch! Stop it!"

The errant dog ducked his head and fell back in step beside her. With the subject of Bryan off limits, we settled into an easy conversation about school gossip. After suffering through the wild emotional mood swings brought on by other people, it was nice walking through the woods with my best friend. I'd always thought of her as an even-keel, peaceful person, but now I had firsthand knowledge to back it up. Her cheerfulness brushed along my skin with soft, steady touches. Only when the dogs did something naughty did they stir, like a pebble in a pool of water. I almost felt normal again.

After making our circuit three times with different sets of dogs, we brought the animals inside for the night, tucking them into their indoor kennels. To my pleasure, Bronwyn didn't mention Bryan again. That was one thing I really loved about her. She never pushed me to talk about things I wanted to avoid.

The peaceful feeling brought on by my best friend was lost the moment I pulled into my driveway. This time, I had no one else to blame for my nervous heart palpitations. Bryan sat on my front steps, the porch light shining down on him as he sat playing some game on his phone. He put it away and stood as I approached.

"Hi, Cady," he said. He genuinely felt miserable. I could feel it pooling in my gut. *Good.*

"Bryan," I replied with a tightness to my voice. I was in no mood to go easy on him, no matter how badly he felt.

He jammed his hands in his pants pockets. "I've been texting you all day."

"I know."

"You didn't reply."

"I didn't read them."

He shook his head and gazed at the ground between our feet. His frustration was making my arms break out in goose bumps.

"Cady, will you just give me a chance to explain?"

I placed my fists on my hips. "Fine. You have exactly one minute, then I'm going in to bed. I've had a long day."

He sighed. "Look, Monica and I dated for a few months before I moved here. It wasn't even all that serious, but we'd been friends before that and when I left, we decided to go back to being just friends."

"But she's flying halfway across the country to go to a stupid dance with you? Yeah, that sounds like just a casual thing a *friend* might do."

Bryan's posture slumped and sparks of annoyance shot out from him. "Before school started, I was miserable here. Didn't know anyone or have anywhere to hang out. I was so bored!" He ran his hand through his hair and blew out a heavy breath from his mouth. "I spent pretty much all of my time on Skype talking to my old friends. Monica had this idea that it might cheer me up to have a date for my first Homecoming here. Her family has money, so it wasn't that big of a deal for her to score airfare to come out for a weekend. I only agreed because I was lonely."

Recalling how lonesome Bryan had appeared that first afternoon in the library, my indignation started to falter.

He must have sensed it, because he stepped forward to take up my hands in his and continued. "She booked the tickets months ago, before I even met you. I'm not even all that into dances and things, but if I have to go, I'd rather it be with you."

The sincerity in his voice was intensified by the warmth in my belly. I hated to admit it, but I could see his point. How could he let this girl come all of the way out to Iowa to see him and not take her to the dance?

"I don't know why you're explaining to me anyway," I said in a huff, "It's not like I have some claim over you."

"You don't?" he asked with a playful grin. "I'd say you have plenty of claim over me." He wrapped his arms around my waist and drew me to his chest.

The proximity of his scent and the warmth of his sentiment won me over. Being in direct contact with his skin made it impossible for me to resist. I lifted my arms up around his shoulders and rested my head on his chest, his heart thumping in time to the waves of affection that he was unknowingly sending through my body. We stood there holding each other and swaying slightly with the breeze for a long moment.

"So," he whispered into my hair, "I think I have a solution for my little dance predicament."

"Hmm?" I replied with my eyes closed so I could concentrate on the beat of his heart.

"Well, I have a plan, but I'll have to fill you in on it later. I need to get home now. My mother wants me there for dinner tonight. Joy. Joy." He rolled his eyes.

"Okay. I'll talk to you later," I said, rising on my tip-toes for a kiss before he left.

Once inside the house, I shucked my shoes and went to the kitchen to fix something to eat. I was squeezing the unnaturally-orange-but-incredibly-tasty cheese into the pot of boiled macaroni when Aaron came bounding up the basement steps.

"Hey," he grunted, dipping his finger through the river of fake cheese and licking it off.

"Ew! You better have clean hands." I shoved him away.

He laughed. "Just took a shower."

His hair was damp.

"Do you want any?" I offered.

"Nah," he said, tying his shoes. "Going over to Trent's house for a Call of Duty marathon."

"Maybe you should try a homework marathon one of these nights."

"You're so funny!" he mocked before running out the door.

I was pouring mac and cheese into a bowl when from upstairs I heard the clatter of shattering glass and the boom of something heavy falling on the floor. *Mom!* Abandoning my bowl, I ran up the steps two at a time and burst into my mom's bedroom without knocking.

"Mom?" I called out. The flickering light coming from the TV was the only light in the room, but I could see her bed was empty, the covers pulled back and resting half on the floor.

A moan sounded from the direction of the closed bathroom door.

I knocked, my other hand poised on the knob, ready to fling it open. Tendrils of fear, self-loathing and pain snaked through from inside, threatening to cut off my breathing, but around the edges of the emotions I detected the fuzziness of intoxication.

"Mom, are you okay? Can I come in?"

I heard her mumble something and then the word "fine." She didn't sound fine. I turned the knob and opened the door.

On the floor next to the shower, my mother was sprawled out naked and dripping blood from dozens of tiny cuts all over her arms, hands and torso. Silvery shards of mirrored glass were scattered on the sink and the tile and glinted off of her skin.

"Holy shit, Mom! What happened?"

"Dun know . . . slip . . . outta nowhere . . ." she mumbled, her eyes glassy and her hands flailing wildly. The wall above the sink held only an empty frame, making the room feel small.

I leaned in, careful not to step on glass in my stocking feet, inspecting her wounds. From my vantage, none looked overly serious, but each trickled several inches of crimson fluid. My mother's eyes drifted closed, and she continued to mumble unintelligibly. She was a mess, but she'd survive.

Frustration began to overtake my worry. I concentrated on bringing my emotional shields up and locking them into place just as Jinx taught me. I knew I'd end up with one heck of a headache later, but I didn't need Mom's depression and drunken stupor killing my post-Bryan buzz.

"Mom, we have to get you out of the glass before you cut yourself more." I reached to help her up, but my hands slipped on the rivers of blood trailing her arms. This wasn't going to work.

"Don't move."

I ran to the bedroom closet where I yanked on a pair of my mother's tennis shoes. Grabbing a pair of slippers and a bathrobe for her, I hurried back to her side.

Mom cried, snot and slobber rolling down over her chin. I bent to put the slippers on her feet. I may have had the right and left mixed up, but at least there would be some protection for when she stood up . . . if I could get her to stand anyway.

My nose wrinkled at the scent of blood and alcohol and unwashed body. With my eyes averted as much as possible from her nakedness, I brushed the loose glass from her skin and wrapped the robe around her. "Come on, Mom, work with me here . . ." I grunted, trying to thread her arms into the sleeves while she continued to fidget.

When she was reasonably covered, I took a towel down from the rack and swept as much of the glass away from her bare legs and bottom as possible.

"I need to get you to the bedroom, Mom. You have to stand and walk." She nodded, but her eyes were closed, and I had doubts whether she really understood.

Standing behind her sitting form, I gripped my mother by the underarms and began to lift. "Mom, stand up. That's right, move your leg . . . no, the other one . . . that's good . . ."

With Herculean effort, I managed to get my mother into her bedroom and deposited onto a reading chair in the corner. She slumped back like a ragdoll, all loose limbed and boneless. The blood was going to completely ruin the powder blue upholstery, but I couldn't care less.

"Stay here," I told her. "I'm going to call 911."

"No!" she yelled.

With the jolt of her fear pounding against my shields, my head snapped around to look at her. The word must have shocked her too because her eyes flashed a moment of lucidity before she collapsed into another fit of sobs.

"Don fine me lik dis," she slurred.

My heart cracked remembering my mother as she used to be, the perfect picture of the career woman, all manicured and styled. Could that really be her slouched in front of me, her bloody robe open, her papery skin hanging on her emaciated skeleton? Had she always been gray? Regular hair appointments ensured I'd never seen her roots before, but now almost an inch of ashy growth framed her face.

No, I couldn't let anyone find her like this.

"Fine, but you have to work with me here. I'll need to inspect your cuts and make sure all of the glass is out. If you make this hard on me or if you need stitches, I'll have to take you in to the hospital. Understand?"

I realized I was talking to her like she was a child, but she nodded and tried to sit up straighter.

"Be right back."

I returned a few minutes later, arms loaded with first-aid items to discover my mother passed out cold in the chair. Maybe it was better this way. I lowered my mental shields, not needing them anymore. A sharp headache immediately ricocheted through my brain, setting my teeth on edge. I took a few deep breaths to steady myself. I turned on the overhead light and dragged over a reading lamp so I could spotlight in on any glints of mirror. Starting at her shoulders and working down I cleansed, disinfected and bandaged. Several times I had to use the tweezers to fish shards from her skin. Thankfully, none of the cuts looked deep enough to require stitches, but she would have lots of scars. I made a mental note to pick her up some of that scar reducing cream next time I went to the grocery store.

At some point during my ministrations, I had to drag my mother to the floor so I could reach her backside. When she was cleaned and wrapped like a mummy, I turned her on her side, tucked a pillow under her head, and covered her with a blanket. I considered cleaning up the mess of blood and glass from the bathroom, but I was tired, my head pounded and part of me wanted her to see the mess she'd made when she sobered up.

# Chapter 22

"I CAN'T BELIEVE I let Bryan talk me into this," Aaron muttered as he straightened his tie in front of the mirror in our foyer. He agreed to the tie after fierce negotiations where I ended up agreeing to write his *Great Expectations* essay. "Who is this chick again?"

"Monica . . . something. She's Bryan's ex-girlfriend," I replied, fiddling with the strap on my heels.

In the days since "the incident" Mom refused to speak about it to me. When I'd come home from school the following day, she was asleep in her bed. A glance into the bathroom showed it to be perfectly clean. In fact, if it weren't for the missing mirror, I might have thought I'd imagined the whole thing. I started to smile, thinking my mom had it together enough to clean up after herself, but then I remembered the house keeper had been there that day. I groaned thinking of the horrible mess left for her. I called my dad and asked him to cut a check for the maid for an additional hundred dollars. He had sort of taken over the whole money thing for the household since Mom obviously wasn't doing it. He agreed to the tip without asking why, a fact for which I was supremely grateful.

Anyway, I hadn't had time to shop for a Homecoming dress, so that morning, after an hour of debating with myself, I'd raided Lony's closet. Her bedroom door had been closed since the funeral, entombing her citrusy scent inside. My heart hurt, as if breaking the seal to her room would somehow allow her spirit to leave us forever.

An eerie feeling snaked up my spine as I took in the familiar bedroom. Several clothing items were strewn across her bed and on the floor, reminding me of the three times she had changed before we'd gone out on the night of her accident. I fingered a cotton sweater on her bed, her first choice of outfit that night, and wondered whether things would've been different had she decided to wear this instead. We might have gotten out of the house ten minutes earlier, met up with her friends ten minutes earlier, maybe gone on the hike through the woods ten minutes earlier. We could have been a mile away from the tracks by the time that train rolled through.

Lony and I have shared clothes our whole lives, so going into her closet shouldn't have bothered me, but it did. I used to yell at her for taking my things without asking. Now, I was the one doing it to her.

"Sorry, Lon," I muttered out loud in case she could hear me on some level.

Lony's closet had enough clothes in it for five people, and all of it stuffed in haphazardly. I rifled through as best as I could until my fingers latched onto a dress that would work. It was the color of lilac blossoms and the fabric was just as delicate. The hem of the tiered skirt just barely reached the knee and the fitted top highlighted my figure. My sister had only worn it once, and that was to Cane's cousin's wedding or something, so I could get away with recycling it for a school event. After a little more digging, I even found a light jacket to pair with it.

Before leaving her room, I stole another glance around. I suppose at some point, my mother would need to get rid of Lony's things, although no one mentioned it yet. My eyes moistened at the thought of all traces of my sister being stripped away in favor of some generic looking guest room.

"I don't know why I even agreed to do this," Aaron complained for the four millionth time. "I hate dances! And things better not get awkward between you and this Monica girl. If this turns into a pissing contest over Bryan, I'm coming back home."

"Don't worry about it," I said, assuring my brother as much as myself. "Bryan says everything will be cool. Maybe you'll even like her."

Aaron sighed and mumbled, "Like that would do me any good with her living across the country."

I rolled my eyes. *Whine much?*

The sound of Bryan's car pulling into my driveway sent me to the mirror to check my hair one last time. I had curled the whole thing and pinned the sides up so that it cascaded down my back like a waterfall. I even put on make-up for the first time in forever. Although I hated to admit it to myself, part of the reason I wanted to look good was so I could hold my own next to Monica.

Aaron opened the door to let Bryan in. He was wearing a pair of black dress pants and a pale green button down shirt with a silver tie. The leather scent from his long, black jacket added to his normal sandalwood, making my head light and fuzzy. In his hands was a small plastic carton containing a corsage.

"Whoa," he whispered. Sparks of happiness jolted off of him, making me blush. *I guess he likes the dress.*

"Thanks. You look nice too."

"Here," he said, getting the corsage out of the carton and tying it around my wrist. It was a white orchid threaded with streaks of purple mounted on a lavender ribbon. Once the bow was secured, Bryan gathered me in his arms for a long, slow kiss. The warmth of his affection ran through my limbs.

"If you two are going to make out all night, I'm staying home," Aaron warned.

I flashed him a dirty look.

"We should go anyway," Bryan replied. "Monica's back at my house. She wasn't quite ready, so I offered to swing back to pick her up on our way to dinner. Besides, my mom wants to meet you."

My heart did a somersault in my chest. *Meet his mother?* Good thing that would be before dinner, so I wouldn't accidentally hurl on her shoes.

Bryan helped me into my jacket, and the three of us walked out to the car.

"Nice ride," Aaron commented with genuine appreciation while sliding into the back of the dark, shiny SUV.

"It's my mother's," Bryan explained, backing out of the drive. "She let me borrow it for the night. I thought it'd be more comfortable. I think it looks like something a Secret Service agent would use to tail the President."

I sank into the leather passenger seat and listened to the boys talk about their favorite cars. I'd never been to Bryan's house before, but I had a pretty good idea from the neighborhood that Bryan's parents had some major cash. His street was lined with huge homes with sprawling, manicured lawns. My nervousness returned as he pulled into a circular driveway in front of a modern, two-story house made of pale brick. The sun had just disappeared over the horizon, but every light in the house was on. These people obviously didn't have to worry about paying their electric bills.

"Wow, you live here?"

"Yeah," Bryan replied with a sigh. He felt embarrassed, but I wasn't sure if that was due to his ostentatious house or his mother standing in the doorway waving at us.

I climbed out of the SUV and straightened my skirt before following Bryan up the walk.

"Mom, this is Cady and her brother Aaron."

"It's nice to meet you both," his mother said with a warm smile. "I've heard so much about you."

"It's nice to meet you too, Mrs. Sullivan," I replied, shaking her cool hand. She was taller than me, but not by much, and her eyes were exactly the same dark pools as Bryan's. Sensing a faint stirring of nerves coming from her went a long way toward easing mine. She wanted to make a good impression on me, too.

"Call me Joan, please." She stepped aside and gestured for us to enter. "Come on in. I told Monica you're here. She'll be right down."

The foyer was as big as my whole bedroom and twice as tall. An open staircase of dark, polished wood stretched up to the second story. It looked like the kind of staircase a Disney princess would float down on in a frothy gown to meet her Prince Charming for the ball. Knowing that was just the entrance that Monica would make soon didn't cheer me at all.

Bryan wrapped his arm loosely around my waist while

Joan made polite conversation with my brother about his college plans. As far as I knew he didn't have any, so I was surprised when he mentioned applying to a graphic design program in Minneapolis.

"I've never seen you in a dress before. You look beautiful," Bryan whispered into my ear, making my neck tingle. "Maybe we could drop Aaron and Monica off at the dance and find some place to be alone."

"Shhh," I replied, my cheeks burning. Not that it didn't sound like a good idea, but the last thing I needed was for his mother to overhear him talking to me that way.

"And how about you, Cady?" Joan asked. "Have you given any thought to college yet?"

I opened my mouth to respond, but the words caught in my throat at the sight of the most gorgeous girl I'd ever seen walking down that fabulous staircase. She was built tall and willowy with legs that went on forever. She wore her blond hair in a short pixie cut, the kind only fashion models could pull off. Her dress was a strapless jade green with a short skirt that might have looked trashy on anyone else, but on her was glamorous.

"Hi," she called out. "Sorry to keep you waiting." She strolled past me to Aaron. "So you must be my date."

Aaron stared at her, corsage in hand and lips parted. You didn't need to be an empath to feel the heat coming off of him. My foot itched to kick him in the shin.

"You're Monica?" he asked, his voice cracking like a thirteen-year-old.

She nodded and gave a sly grin. "I sure am. Is that for me?"

Aaron looked at the corsage in his hands as if he didn't know how it had gotten there. "Uh, yeah."

Her corsage was one meant to be pinned to the dress, meaning the only place to attach it was directly above her breast. His fingers fumbled with the pin, obviously struggling to keep his mind out of the gutter and on the task at hand. The combination of his terror and arousal was making my hands tremble. Monica seemed to be enjoying his discomfort a little too much for my tastes.

"Let me do that before you stab yourself," I said, stepping forward to take the pin out of his hand. Aaron looked relieved.

I stood in front of Monica uneasily while she grinned down at me. She had to be at least five foot ten and in her heels, she towered over me. Her feeling of superiority made my jaw clench. The differences between us were glaringly obvious, and I didn't appreciate having to look up to speak to her.

"Here you go," I said, securing the flower to her dress.

"Thanks," she replied, refocusing on my brother. I knew I'd been dismissed.

I stepped back to my place beside Bryan again, needing to get some distance from Monica's vibes of over confidence. Seeing me, she obviously didn't feel any need to worry. It made me wonder if she truly was over Bryan or if she just didn't see me as competition.

I didn't have to wait long to find out the answer. When Monica turned her gaze on Bryan, I was struck by a heady combination of desire, jealousy and yes —a little bit of love. Not that her face betrayed any of this. Monica's lips curled into a cool smile. Her passion made me feel like vomiting.

"So, Bryan," she said, "Aren't you going to introduce us?"

A ripple of tension rolled off of him. "Oh, yeah. This is

Cady. Cady, this is my friend, Monica."

"Nice to meet you," I choked out, hoping my plastic grin didn't look too unnatural. Monica surveyed me and that annoying confidence came raging back. My belly tightened with humiliation.

"Well, should we go?" She said it like a question, but we all sort of knew it was a command. Monica slipped a silk jacket on, and we all followed her out of the house like lemmings. Bryan's mom waved to us from the door as we pulled out of the drive.

Neither Bryan nor I said much on the way to the Italian restaurant where he had reserved a table for us. Monica prattled on in the back seat, asking my brother questions like she was interested in him, but I knew it was for show. I can't explain it really, but I could feel her trying to make Bryan jealous. She would be looking Aaron in the eyes and smiling at him as he spoke, but the waves of her emotions were rolling toward Bryan. It was the first time I realized I could actually sense the direction of the vibrations, adding a whole new level of insight for me. As far as I could tell, Bryan didn't seem to be reacting to her. He held my hand, stroking his guitar calloused thumb in slow circles on the back of my hand, and watched the road.

At the restaurant, we followed the hostess to a table in the back corner of the room. Bryan gave me a reassuring grin as he held my chair out for me. I took a deep breath to clear the tension in my chest. *Bryan likes me,* I told myself. *I have nothing to worry about.*

The restaurant was busy, about half of the customers being other kids going out before Homecoming. It was a popular date option for students because the atmosphere was elegant, but the prices weren't too high. Bryan waved at a couple of guys from the jazz band, and Aaron excused himself for a minute to go talk to Trent, who was there with some sophomore girl.

Monica was seated directly in front of me. I already knew what I wanted to order, but I scanned the menu anyway to keep from watching her. Monica didn't bother opening hers. The weight of her stare was making me itch.

"So, Cady," she said, her tone dripping with friendliness, "Bryan hasn't told me anything about you. What's your story?"

I wasn't sure what to say. My mind was completely blank, and I'm sure it showed on my face. Luckily, Bryan rescued me.

"Cady is the first friend I made when school started," he explained. "We have a class together, but she never noticed me. For days, I stared at the back of her head and wanted to talk to her, but then I literally ran into her in the library. Not my smoothest move, but she didn't hold it against me."

My heart warmed at his admission that he was interested in me even before we officially met. Maybe I really didn't have anything to worry about with Monica.

"Did Bryan ever tell you how he and I met?" she asked.

*Bryan never mentioned you,* I thought to myself. "No, he didn't."

"We were only about seven years old. Our fathers were both working for the same investment firm at the time, and his family came over to our Fourth of July picnic. He was this scrawny little thing who wouldn't talk." She laughed with her mouth open, showing her pearly teeth.

Bryan gave her a mock glare, but then smiled. "I told you," he explained to me. "I was home schooled, so I didn't have a lot of experience with other kids, much less with girls."

"So, my sister and I thought it'd be fun to dress him up," she continued. "We took him up to our room and made him put on this little yellow dress. We clipped barrettes in his hair and put on some of our mother's lipstick. We wanted blush too, but couldn't find any, so we smudged the lipstick on his cheeks. He looked like some warped version of a drag queen!"

"Don't listen to her," he said squeezing my hand lightly. "I looked hot."

"I bet you did," I replied, rolling my eyes.

"When we had him all dressed up, we wanted to make a big production about showing him off, so my sister, who was like ten at the time got out her portable CD player and her Grease Soundtrack —"

"Yeah, yeah," Bryan interrupted. "They made me parade around the backyard in front of everyone to the song 'Look at Me, I'm Sandra Dee.' Real hilarious."

I had to admit, it was funny, and I giggled along with Monica.

"My brother never let me live that down either," he muttered.

Aaron returned to our table just as the waiter appeared. I ordered the veggie lasagna which came in a slice almost as large as the plate. Monica got a Caesar salad with the dressing on the side. She would dunk her fork in the dressing before stabbing her lettuce. I guess I understood now how she was so thin.

After dinner, we headed over to the high school. The cafeteria was transformed by the magic of the school Spirit Committee. The tables had all been folded away, leaving only some folding chairs in different areas of the room for people to sit in when they got sick of dancing. The florescent lights were off, the only illumination coming from thousands of white Christmas lights laced around the ceiling and dripping down the walls. A long table at one end had punch and soda being served by some student volunteers, and a couple strategically placed bins of dry ice sent billows of fog rolling over the floor.

"Do you dance?" Monica shouted to Aaron over the up-tempo pop music.

He nodded, taking her hand and leading her out to the dance floor. I'd never seen my brother dance before, but he managed to pull it off without looking any worse than anyone else. Monica undulated next to him, a little too closely.

Across the room, I spotted a photographer taking pictures of the couples. "Let's get our picture taken." I suggested.

"Sure," Bryan shrugged.

Walking across the room, I tensed up at the onslaught of emotions coming from the crowd. Luckily, most of the students were in good moods. When I got within range of the dancers though, the elation coming off of them made my head dizzy. I clutched Bryan's arm. The direct contact helping to filter some of the emotional pollution out.

"You okay?" he yelled.

I nodded and led him away from the dancers.

"Are you sure?" he asked. "You looked like you were going to faint for a minute there. Do you want me to get you something to drink?"

My body was still a little woozy. "Just some punch, I think."

"Be right back."

Bryan threaded his way through the crowd, while I

staked a claim on the wall. This was only the second dance I'd been to, and the only semi-formal. Lony had made me go with her to the back-to-school dance at the beginning of our freshman year. It was okay until she latched onto some cute boy and left me alone for the rest of the night.

I spotted Shawn and Angelique coming toward me from the dance floor. They were both breathing heavy and damp with sweat. Shawn was dressed like a 1920's gangster and Angelique wore a vintage flapper dress, complete with the matching headband wrapped around her forehead.

"Hey, girl!" Shawn called out. "Where'd your hot date go?"

"To get me something to drink. You guys having fun?"

Angelique draped her arm around Shawn's shoulders. "Are you kidding? This DJ is incredible! Every song he has played so far has been killer!"

"How're your brother and the ex getting along?" Shawn asked, after Angelique excused herself to use the restroom.

I gestured for him to take a look for himself. Aaron and Monica were wrapped up in each other grinding like they've been lovers for years. Aaron had this stupid grin on his face like he won the lottery or something. I gave them five minutes before some chaperone went over and broke them up.

"Whoa!" Shawn replied. "She's cute."

"She's more than cute," I pointed out honestly, unable to mask the hostility in my voice. "She still has the hots for Bryan too."

"Did she say something to you?"

"She didn't have to," I answered. "Call it intuition."

Bryan returned holding two plastic cups of pink punch. I sniffed and noticed right away that someone had spiked it. *Oh, well*, I thought, raising it to my lips and drinking it anyway. The strawberry liquid burned down my throat.

"Woah, that's strong!" Bryan exclaimed after gulping his down.

"Yeah, I saw a few of the football players dumping Smirnoff in the bowl a while ago," said Shawn.

We talked for a few minutes more before Angelique returned and danced Shawn away.

Bryan took my empty cup and tossed it with his into the garbage. "Come on. Let's get our picture taken."

We walked over to the photography area and stood in the short line. When our turn came up, we positioned ourselves in front of a light blue backdrop and posed with our arms around each other. I knew from seeing other people's homecoming pictures in the past that they always turned out cheesy, but I didn't care. I was happy having Bryan by my side for the whole school to see.

A slow song came on and the crowd on the dance floor changed. New couples rotating in to rock back and forth with their dates as those who came stag sloughed off to find something to drink.

"Wanna dance?" Bryan asked.

I nodded and let him lead me out by the hand. I kept us on the edge of the crowd and my body in direct contact with his, so I wouldn't be overcome by the emotions of the crowd again. Bryan pulled me into his arms, and I rested my head on his chest where I could hear his heart beat in time to the music.

Being so close blocked out the vibrations from the others, allowing me to tap fully into him. The same calm glow that I was used to from Bryan was there, but also something else, something that made my pulse quicken and caused me to press against him tighter. I let out a little gasp when I felt the evidence of what it was.

My body stirred in response to his, and I lifted my lips to meet his. His fingers roamed lightly over the exposed skin on my back and down my side. Our breathing turned shallow.

"Oh, Bryan," I moaned as I pressed myself against him and rode the waves of his closeness.

"Thank you for coming with me tonight," he said into my ear, his hot breath sending a shiver down my neck. "I hated the idea of having to take Monica."

"Why?" I asked, "She's gorgeous. All of the guys would've been jealous of you."

Bryan shrugged. "She's pretty, but she's not you." Bryan drew back to look me in the eyes. "I'm being honest here . . . I dated her because she was fun, but I never felt for her what I feel for you." His hands tightened on my waist and his expression seemed to be waiting for a response. My head spun with the headiness of it all.

"I haven't dated much," I admitted. "But I've never liked anyone as much as I like you either."

His mouth broke into a grin, and he bent to kiss me again.

After two slow songs, the DJ went back to fast ones, so we left the dance floor. My head swam as if intoxicated by him. Bryan steered me over to introduce me to Jeff and Tim, his friends from the jazz band. I remembered Tim from a biology class we had together the year before. He had a reputation for being a talented guitarist, and I'd heard he played in a band with some college guys. Tim's date, Kelly Locke, lives down the street from me. We used to play with each other sometimes when we were kids. I didn't catch the name of the mousey-looking girl standing next to Jeff. Her discomfort and self-consciousness was killing my buzz.

"What're you guys doing after this?" Tim asked. "My parents are gone for the weekend, so I'm having a few people over. You can stop by if you want."

Bryan looked at me and shrugged.

"I don't think I really have a curfew," I said. "My mom never notices me coming or going lately."

"Okay, maybe we'll stop by then," Bryan told him. Tim texted Bryan his address.

The music paused after a song, and a little screech of feedback alerted me to the girl standing on a raised platform trying to get everyone's attention.

"Excuse me!" she called out. It was Vanessa Moriarty, the Homecoming Queen and one of Lony's cheerleading friends. "Can I have your attention?"

The room quieted to a low murmur.

"I'd like to take a few minutes to remember my good friend, Avalon Day, who tragically passed away in September."

I groaned and Bryan took my hand.

"The tradition of Homecoming is one where students and alumni come together to celebrate our alma mater," she read off an index card. "This year, Lony's missing presence has affected us all. She was one of the nicest girls I've ever known, so fun and full of life. That's why the Senior High cheer squad has put together a short memorial slide show to honor her memory. We'll follow the show with a moment of silence."

One of the cheerleaders rolled a projector out and shined it on a large screen hung against the wall. A shot of Lony's sophomore yearbook picture flashed up and Sarah McLaughlin's "I Will Remember You" started to play.

"I think I'm going to go to the bathroom," I said to Bryan.

"Are you okay?" His concern lapping at my mind.

"I'm fine, really. I just need to walk. I'll be back."

# Chapter 23

ISLIPPED OUT the cafeteria door into the brightly lit hallway. Instead of going into the bathroom though, I headed out of the side doors toward an outdoor seating area. I sucked in the fresh night air and hugged my arms to fend off the autumn chill. Since the school sits on top of a hill, I had a pretty good view of the city lights.

A shuffle sound to my left caught my attention. I peeked around the corner of the building and saw the silhouette of a guy sitting on the grass alone, his face buried in his hands. I was too far away to judge his emotions, but I thought something might be wrong.

I walked slowly toward him. When I got within fifteen feet, he must have heard my footsteps and his head snapped up. It was Cane Matthews.

He jumped to his feet and held the wall of the school for support. He appeared to be tipsy. The expression on his face was one of shock, all round, glassy eyes and paleness. His mouth opened as if to say something, but no words came out.

"Cane . . ." I said, not knowing what to say to him. Ever since the accident, I got the distinct impression that he hated me, or at least hated looking at me.

"Oh, Cady," he replied breathlessly. "You scared me. You're wearing her dress."

For the briefest of moments, he must have thought I was my sister. I continued walking forward, but once I stepped within range of his emotions, my stomach clenched up so tightly that I almost doubled over. He was a one-man hurricane of sorrow. I would've expected sadness, but the overwhelming guilt shocked me. *What does he have to feel guilty about?* My hands shook and the muscles in my shoulders compressed.

"It hurts to look at you," he said, stepping up so close I could smell the booze on his breath. He reached up with his finger and traced my bottom lip.

"I'm sorry," I whispered, although whether I meant I was sorry for my looks or sorry for his loss, I couldn't tell.

"I always thought you were prettier though," he continued, his words slurring slightly. "Bet you never knew that. You're so natural and carefree. Lony was so . . . *polished*." He spit it out like a dirty word.

I trembled under the weight of the icy waves coming off his skin, and his drunkenness was making me dizzy. I thought about blocking him, but I didn't want to give myself a blinding migraine and ruin the rest of my night.

Cane tightened his fists by his sides. "Don't get me wrong, I cared about your sister. *I did.* But I just couldn't do it anymore. I couldn't take the fighting all the time."

"W-what are you saying, Cane?"

He didn't answer right away. His green eyes glazed with alcohol roamed over my face as if committing it to memory.

Finally, he whispered, "I did something unforgivable."

*What in the hell is he talking about?* My abdominal muscles ached from the tension between us, and pressure built up behind my eyes. I put my hand on the bricks of the building to keep myself upright and allowed my mind to flick back to that night.

I could see them walking along the tracks. I couldn't hear their words, but Lony was gesturing wildly. She kept stopping like she wanted him to also, but he never did. He kept walking ahead of her with his hands jammed in his pockets, so she would have to rush to catch up. When the headlight on the train swept around the corner, both faces looked up in shock. At that point, a good twenty feet separated them. Cane moved first, jumping off the tracks. When Lony stood frozen, he turned back yelling at her to move. Lony snapped out of it and tried to flee, but her sandal caught on a rail and she fell down. Cane ran back toward her, but he was too late.

I squeezed my eyes to keep the tears from escaping. "Cane, I saw it. I remember every detail. You are not responsible for Lony getting hit by the train."

He shook his head. His drunken dizziness slipped over me, making my head spin.

"You don't understand," he argued through clenched teeth, tugging on his hair in frustration. Now, anger filled him, adding to the mix. The cold burn of it filled my veins with ice water, causing me to hold the wall of the building for support. Cane turned on his heel and started in the direction of the parking lot.

"Cane, wait!" I yelled.

When he ignored me, I ran after him as quickly as my delicate shoes would allow, catching up to him just as he approached his truck. I grabbed his wrist as he reached for the door handle.

Cane spun me around and pressed my back up against the cold metal door. One arm was wrapped around my back, clutching my hair with his fist. The other hand pressed against the driver door, trapping me in place.

"It should have been me!" he hissed, his eyes moist with unshed tears.

The ferocity of his emotions froze me to the bone. My teeth chattered audibly.

"I fucked up, and it should have been me. If I hadn't . . ." He trailed off.

"If you hadn't *what*, Cane?" my voice shook. "There was nothing you could have done. What, do you wish you would've thrown yourself on the tracks too?"

"Maybe I should have! She didn't deserve to die like that, with her heart broken."

"What are you talking about?" My body trembled with the cold pulsing off of him. My headache was reaching migraine levels and causing my vision to blur. I couldn't have blocked him now if I tried.

"I broke up with her," Cane said through gritted teeth. "I told her that it was over, that I didn't love her."

I gasped, but couldn't form any words.

"We were walking behind you guys, and she started in on me because she thought I was paying more attention to Carly Smith in the parking lot than to her." His grip on my hair relaxed a bit, but he didn't let me go.

I remembered the red-head from the parking lot.

"Lon was just mad because Carly and I know people that she didn't, and she felt excluded by our conversation. I get that, but we'd been having the same sort of arguments repeatedly for months, and I was tired of it. Just because I talk to another girl, it doesn't mean I'm interested in them. Carly is my second cousin, by the way, not that Lony asked before jumping to conclusions."

Talking about that night seemed to be helping him, and I wondered if I was the first person he admitted any of this to. I had the distinct impression that I was somehow absorbing his anger. The waves of his emotions were still as cold, but were coming less intense now. Only in the places where he touched me did I feel any warmth at all. I leaned against him, drawn like a cat to a sunny spot.

"So, you broke up with her?"

"Yes," he admitted. He bent to rest his forehead against mine. "I'm so sorry, Cady. I'm so sorry she had to die knowing that I didn't want her anymore. And then people were so supportive and nice to me thinking I'd lost my girlfriend. It made everything a million times worse."

I wasn't sure how I felt about Cane's confession. On one hand, the thought of Lony's last moments being ones of pain broke my heart. I thought back to those minutes that I'd experienced before passing out. I remember that feeling of loss. At the time, I thought it was the loss of her life that had her so sorrowful, but now, I could see a whole different side to what must have been going through her head.

But another part of me understood how Cane felt and longed to comfort his sorrow away. Lony's death was not his fault, and he'd had every right to break up with her if he wanted to. I never understood how they handled all of the stress from their bickering anyway. Perhaps it was due to the contact of our bodies making the emotional connection between us so strong, but I could feel how his guilt was tearing him up inside. I couldn't be angry with him for hurting my sister. Not when he was hurting too. I reached my arms around his shoulders to pull him to me. He crumpled against me, burying his face into my shoulder.

After a moment, my friendly hug turned into a different kind of embrace. The full length of him was pressed against me, trapping me between his muscled body and the steel door of his truck. Our breathing grew shallow, and I was too aware of our hearts beating in unison. For the second time that night, my traitorous body echoed the stirrings of another's arousal. The heat of his growing passion flowed through me, awakening a need deep in my belly. My mouth dropped open in shock just as Cane leaned in and kissed me deeply. I couldn't fight my body's response to his hot mouth, faintly tasting of vodka. For one moment, I allowed myself to kiss him back, letting my tongue match the rhythmic movements of his, trailing my fingers down the strong plane of his broad back. The feedback of our completed circuit of emotions threatened to carry me away . . . until I remembered Bryan. I brought my fists up to push against Cane's chest.

"Stop!" I cried, twisting my body to get out from the jail of his arms.

Cane snapped his head back in surprise as if just realizing what he did. The drunken glaze was completely gone from his eyes. He let go of me and stumbled back.

"Oh, Jesus, Cady. I'm sorry!"

Both of us had tears in our eyes. I felt a new remorse flood in alongside his original guilt. Without the heat of his body, the sharp coldness returned making my insides shiver.

"It's all right, Cane." I reached for his arm to comfort him, but he flinched away. Suddenly, an emotion hit me in the chest, causing me to stumble back against the truck. The freeze was so intense that when I gasped, a plume of fog came out of my mouth. Even if I had not been able to feel it, one look at Cane's face told me what it was . . . self-hatred.

He shoved me out of the way and climbed into his pick-up.

"Cane, I don't think you're in any condition to drive." I tried to reach for his keys, but he slammed the door in my face.

"Cane!" I yelled, beating on the window with my fists. "Don't go! At least let me drive you!"

He lowered the window and fixed a hostile glare on me. "What? Are you afraid I'll get into an accident? Maybe kill myself? It's no less than I deserve."

"Don't talk like that! If you want to go home, I'll take you. Let me in."

"No, Cady. Home's the last place I want to go." With that he closed the window and threw the truck in gear. He tore out of the parking lot, his wheels spinning a black mark on the pavement.

I stood there immobile, my body rapidly warming with him out of my presence. But I couldn't let Cane go off like that. What if he hurt himself? I tried to concentrate on whether any of his emotions indicated he was suicidal, but I couldn't tell. Once again, I cursed the fact that my abilities didn't allow me to read minds like Jinx. *Jinx!* I turned and ran to the building. The high school was on the edge of her range, but Cane must have been broadcasting loud enough for her to pick up on his thoughts in the parking lot.

Back inside the dance, the flashing lights and hard thumping bass attacked my aching head. Across the room, Bryan looked surprised when he saw me rush in, but I ignored him and ran straight to the coat racks to fish my cell phone out of my pocket.

"Cady, what's wrong?" Bryan asked, coming up alongside me.

Ignoring his concern, I dialed Jinx's number. "Crap! I can't hear in here!"

I rushed back to the doors with Bryan on my heels.

"Jinx! Can you hear me?" I asked, tears springing to my eyes. I blinked them away before they could spill.

"Not sure if he's suicidal or not," she answered without me having to ask the question, "but he's headed out to the Mines of Spain."

"Oh, no!" I said, "He's been drinking. He could get hurt out there."

"Do you want me to take you out to get him?"

I looked over at Bryan. "No, I'll have Bryan take me. Thanks." I hung up. Turning to Bryan, "Cane's in trouble, and someone needs to go get him."

Bryan nodded. "Let me go get Aaron and Monica."

# Chapter 24

BRYAN DISAPPEARED BACK inside the dance. Sobs clawed at the back of my throat, but I refused to give in to them. My body shook from the wild physical changes it had experienced with Cane. I rolled my neck to loosen up my shoulders, but the knots were in there solid.

I couldn't believe Cane kissed me. Even worse? I couldn't believe I kissed him back! What came over me? It was almost like I'd had no control over myself, but at the same time, it was all me. For that one moment, I wanted him. I couldn't dwell on it though because just then Bryan returned carrying both of our jackets, Aaron and Monica right behind him.

Aaron's face clouded with concern when he saw me trembling. "You okay? What's going on?"

"I'll tell you in the car." I promised as we jogged off to the vehicle.

Once in the passenger seat, I turned the heat up full blast

202

and pulled on my jacket. My teeth chattered uncontrollably. The fact that everyone else in the car was all keyed up and confused wasn't helping me calm down.

"Head toward the Mines of Spain," I instructed. Bryan nodded and turned south.

"Why?" Aaron demanded. "I don't think that's a very good idea. It's too dark and you don't look steady enough to go tromping through the woods."

I quickly told them about Cane's state of mind and that he'd been drinking. Aaron still didn't like the idea of me going after him, but he shut his mouth and didn't try to talk me out of it.

"Are *you* okay?" Bryan asked, real concern showing in his eyes, brushing my skin with a loving coolness. I nodded, but the concern in his eyes fueled my guilt. I really liked this boy, but I kissed someone else not fifteen minutes earlier. Not just anyone, but my dead sister's boyfriend. The cramping in my belly had nothing to do with the emotions of the other passengers in the vehicle.

At a stop light, Bryan reached over and grasped my hand. "Jesus, your hands are freezing!" He raised his hand to touch my burning cheek. "I think you have a fever."

"I'll be okay in a few minutes," I replied. My trembling had nearly stopped, but I felt light headed. I guess when emotions were strong enough, they could affect my physical body, not just my emotional barometer. I made a mental note to ask Jinx about it.

When we got to the parking lot on the edge of the woods, Cane's truck was parked at an odd angle and he was nowhere in sight.

"What an idiot," Aaron muttered, running his hand

through his hair. "You said he was drinking?"

I nodded.

"Okay, you girls stay here. Bryan and I will go look for him."

Before I had a chance to protest, Monica piped up. "Who are you, Fred Flintstone? Cady and I are not waiting here like helpless little girls."

"That's right," I added. "We can cover more ground if we split up into groups."

Bryan didn't look happy about it, but he reluctantly nodded. "There should be a flashlight in my glove box. I've never been here before, but I assume you and Aaron are both familiar enough, right?"

"Sure," I nodded. "Give Aaron and Monica the flashlight. They can go deeper into the trees. If we stick to the trail that goes along the cliff base, we should be able to get along all right. When it gets closer to the Mississippi, the trees thin out, so that'll give us some moonlight."

The four of us climbed out of the car and set off down separate paths. My body was mostly recovered from Cane's emotional freeze. I clung to Bryan's arm as we walked as fast as I could in my dress shoes. Thankfully, it hadn't rained in a while, so the ground was hard and dry. Still, I stumbled along in the dark.

"Cane!" I called out. "Where are you?"

In the distance I could hear echoes of Aaron and Monica calling out also. If Cane could hear us, he wasn't inclined to answer.

A break in the trees ahead illuminated a fork in the path. To the left was a steep incline leading up to the trails along the rocky bluffs. The right path wound around the base toward the river. It was the same trail I'd walked the night of my sister's death. I felt a little sick to my stomach at the memory and quickly stuffed it down into a back compartment in my mind.

"You don't think he would have gone up there, do you?" Bryan asked.

I shook my head. "He's not that stupid. The trails get rocky and it's too easy to slide around. It's not all that safe during the daylight, but at night, it's treacherous."

We continued on, calling out to Cane as we walked. I could still hear Aaron and Monica, but their calls were getting more distant. When we reached the clearing before the river, I stopped short.

"What is it?" Bryan asked.

I cleared my throat. "I-I just haven't been back here, you know?"

"Is this . . . ?"

I nodded, pointing a shaky finger toward the train tracks. "Those are the tracks. I was with some people sitting by those boulders over there. We were waiting for Lony and Cane to catch up. She was hit right about there."

"I'm sorry," he said, wrapping a comforting arm around my shoulders. "Maybe we should turn around and go another direction. Cane isn't down this far."

I stood silent looking ahead at the tracks. I don't know why it never occurred to me to visit this place before now. I never believed in things like ghosts and spirits before, but meeting Jinx and discovering that I'm an empath suddenly had me questioning everything. Maybe there was something of Lony still lingering here. I sure as heck never felt her presence at home.

"Can you give me a minute?"

Bryan kissed me on my forehead and let go of my shoulders.

I could walk a little easier now that there was more moonlight visible. I drew my jacket tight across my chest, more for comfort than cold. The long, weedy grass gradually gave way to gravel which rose up a short bank to the gleaming steel tracks. To my left, I spotted an area where the grass was more matted down. I walked over and found a patch of gravel a shade brighter than the rest. *This must be the place,* I thought. *New gravel to replace the stuff covered in blood.*

I knelt down on the rocks, not caring about the sharp pains in my knees. I placed my hand on the cold rail.

"Lony," I whispered. "I feel like I never got a real chance to say good bye to you. In some ways, I still can't believe you're gone. Nothing's the same anymore." I swiped a lone tear off of my cheek.

"Cane told me about what happened, about the break up. I'm so sorry. I know how much you cared about him —how much you probably still do care about him wherever you are. He isn't doing so well, Lon. The guilt is eating him up inside. That's why I'm here tonight. I want to help him. Somehow, I know that's what you'd want me to do. And don't worry, I'll take better care of Mom and Dad, too. I promise. I love you."

I closed my eyes and reached out with my senses, but there was nothing in my range to connect with. Part of me had been hoping that if Lony's spirit was still here, I would be able to feel her with my mind. Nothing.

"Cady!" Bryan cried. "I think I see him!"

Rising to my feet, I wiped the dirt from my knees. I looked back to see Bryan pointing up to the bluff. A figure was stumbling around, well off of the trail, on the side of the rocky face.

*"Cane!"* I yelled.

The person on the bluff looked in my direction. "Cady? I can't get down!"

I ran back to Bryan. "He's gonna fall!" I exclaimed.

Bryan shrugged off his jacket and handed it to me. Next, he stripped off the tie.

"What are you doing?"

"I'm going up there after him," Bryan answered, rolling up his sleeves. "Stay here."

"No!" I protested, but Bryan ignored me and began picking his way up the steep incline.

As much as I wanted to go after him, I knew I'd never make it in my shoes.

"Cane, don't move!" I yelled up to him. "Bryan's coming." I wasn't even sure if Cane knew who Bryan was, but now wasn't the time for introductions.

I withdrew my phone from my pocket and called Aaron. "We found him, but the idiot is stuck up on the bluff. Bryan is going to help him down."

Aaron muttered a curse. "Tell me where you are."

"It's the bluff bordering the river and the tracks. East-side."

Aaron hung up with a promise to be there soon.

"Aaron's on his way," I called up.

Cane leaned against the limestone rock, his fingers clutching the crevices. I hoped the river view from fifty-feet-high would help to sober him up. Bryan reached the trail along the side of the bluff and was using it to get as close to Cane as possible. At the closest point, he began picking his way in Cane's direction.

"I'm almost there," Bryan called out, his voice echoing between the bluffs. Only a few feet separated them now, but each step closer ran the risk of their rocky footholds giving way. Bryan found a tiny tree growing out from the cracks of the rocks and yanked on it. Seeing that it was secure, he used it as an anchor as he stretched out toward Cane.

"Almost there. Give me your hand."

Cane shifted to his left and grasped Bryan's hand.

"I gotcha," Bryan grunted, holding Cane steady and directing him back toward the trail. I didn't realize I was holding my breath until they made it to the relative safety of the trail, and I let it out with a gush. *They're safe.*

"Just follow the path," I called up. "I'll meet you back at the fork."

I entered the darkness of the woods again. Without Bryan there to steady me on me, I tripped on rocks and had to cling to passing branches to keep from falling. Under the loud chirping of frogs and crickets, I could hear the guys off to my right, still quite a ways up, but I couldn't make out their words. Briefly, I let myself think about that kiss with Cane in the parking lot. Shame filled my lungs as I remembered pressing myself to his warmth and kissing him back. *What was I thinking?* I chastised myself. *How could I do that to Bryan? Especially after the way I reacted over Monica!*

I was going to have to tell him, but how would I ever explain? *Oh, Bryan. I am some sort of weird psychic who can read emotions, and sometimes I get tangled up in what other people are feeling.* Yeah, that'd go over well.

Why did Cane have to go and kiss me anyway? I get that he was distraught, but what made him go there? Maybe it was because I reminded him so much of my sister. I guess he just got caught up in the heat of the moment and wasn't thinking clearly, but at the time, it hadn't felt that way. There was something real in that kiss, at least from his side. I found myself hoping that Cane would forget about it once he sobered and never mention it to me again.

I stopped to pick a rock from my shoe when I heard surprised yells and the racket of rocks crashing to the ground.

"Bryan! Cane! Are you okay?" I shouted.

"No!" Cane called out, pain evident in his voice. "Help, Cady, quick!"

I left the path and rushed through the brush in the direction of the voices. Brambles and branches scratched at my legs, snagging my dress, but I pressed on as fast as I could. I reached the base of the cliff and saw Bryan and Cane lying on the ground. Cane's leg was bent at an unnatural angle below the knee, and Bryan was bleeding from a huge gash on his side. Bleeding heavily.

All of the blood drained from my head. Huge waves of icy pain vibrated off of the guys, stabbing me in the gut. Between the crazy emotions emanating from them and the tinny scent of blood in the air, my stomach roiled with nausea.

"Bryan!" I cried, rushing to him and dropping to my knees by his side.

"I slipped," Cane explained through clenched teeth, "and he tried to grab me, but then we both came down."

Bryan's expression was one of sheer horror as he tore open his shirt to inspect the damage. The rip in his skin started just below his back shoulder, cut across his ribs and reached nearly down to his waistband. Even in the darkness, I knew it was deep enough to expose his ribs bones.

"What do I do?" I cried, pressing his coat to his side to hold in the freely flowing blood.

Bryan looked at me. We both had tears in our eyes. "I don't think there's time to do anything," he whispered with finality.

An agonizing noise tore out of me as I realized there was no way he could ever survive an injury this huge. The terror between us was so strong that I couldn't tell where mine ended and Bryan's began.

"You can't die! I won't let you!"

Bryan's face was already pale and the blood was leaking through the jacket onto the ground.

"He's dying?" Cane asked confused.

"I have . . . hemophilia." he tried to explain, breathing in sharp heaves. He leaned back on his elbow, getting weaker.

"Oh my god!" came a shriek from behind me.

Aaron and Monica stood a few feet behind us, having followed our voices to our location. Monica's eyes were as large as moons at the sight of the blood. She understood the seriousness of the situation. She dropped to her knees and began sobbing into her hands.

Aaron took off his coat and handed it to me. I dropped Bryan's soaked jacket and replaced it with fresh, soft cotton, still warm from my brother's body heat.

"I'm calling 911," Aaron said taking out his phone.

"There's no time!" Over the wound, my hands vibrated wildly with icy stabs of pain. I recognized the feeling from when I had detected the tumor on Lucy, only this time it was a hundred times more intense.

"Cady . . . n-nothing you can do," Bryan choked out, dropping to lie on his back. "Just h-happy you're . . . with me."

"Don't do that! Don't you say good bye to me!"

My hands burned from the freezing pain. Instinctively, I threw up my mental shields and began to press back. That's when I noticed warmth flooding down my arms into my hands and radiating out from my fingertips. I let my heated hands hover directly over the wound, focusing all my energy on willing it away. The trickle of blood began to slow to a stop, and I feared it meant the end, but Bryan was still conscious and breathing thick wheezy breaths. Determination and love swelled in my chest, as I concentrated on that open wound. Bryan sucked in a sharp gasp.

"W-what are you doing?" he asked. "It tingles . . . warm."

I flexed my mind and concentrated harder. Heat vibrated out from my hands and the flesh began to knit itself back together before my eyes.

"Holy shit!" Cane exclaimed, watching as the wound closed into a jagged raised scar.

I fell backward and rested my head hit the ground. My breath heaved as if I'd just run a marathon. My head pounded with every beat of my heart.

Bryan sat up and ran his hands along the seam in his skin. "It's healed. Doesn't even hurt."

Monica looked up, mascara running down her cheeks. "Wha . . . ?" She crawled close enough to get a look, managing to avoid the sticky puddle that I was now half-lying in.

"Cady?" my brother said in confusion. He snapped his phone closed, his eyes darting between me and the closed wound.

"What did she do to you, man?" Cane asked. He tried to lean in to get a better look, but winced and gripped his leg.

I drew myself back to my knees, head swimming, and scooted over to inspect Cane's knee. His pant leg was already ripped, but I tore the hole further to get a better look. The skin was scraped and embedded with pebbles and dirt, but not bleeding too badly. The knee was twisted and bent about 45 degrees in an impossible direction. It had to be broken. No way could a normal leg form an angle like that.

"There goes my college scholarships," he muttered.

I wasn't sure if he meant it as a poor attempt at humor or not, but he spoke the truth. Not only did Cane play football, but he also ran track and was the school star pitcher on the baseball team. Everyone assumed he would end up going to a Big Ten school on a sports scholarship. Some people even had hopes for him playing professionally someday. From the looks of things, that dream was over.

I placed my hand over the knee and felt around with my senses. Cold stabs of pain flicked my palms. "It's pretty bad, but I can't fix it like this. We have to get it straight first."

Cane's eyes got round as he realized the pain that would be involved with setting the leg.

I wasn't sure I *could* fix it. I didn't even know how exactly I'd managed to heal Bryan. But I had to try. I had to ignore my weak, trembling body and try.

My hands ran across the cool ground until I found a broken branch. I snapped off the end and dusted the loose dirt away.

"Put this between your teeth," I instructed Cane. "Aaron, can you give me a hand?"

My brother knelt down by Cane's feet.

"When I say so, I want you to take hold of his ankle and pull that leg straight." Amazingly, my brother didn't question my authority, just gritted his teeth in sympathy, and clutched Cane's ankle with both hands.

"You want to set his broken leg?" Monica shrieked, then turning to Cane, "And you're going to let her?"

Bryan set his hand on her shoulder and murmured something about calming down.

I looked at Cane and asked, "Well? Are you going to let me try? I can't guarantee anything, but it's your decision."

Cane's chest was rising and falling so rapidly, I was afraid he'd hyperventilate. His fear caused my palms to sweat and the muscles to tighten in my limbs.

"I-I saw what you did . . . to him," his eyes flitted over toward Bryan face still pale, but from what we could tell, looked to be healed. Cane turned his gaze back to me, trying to focus through his pain. "I tr-trust you."

"Okay, then," I said sliding closer. "You have to force yourself to relax, Cane, or I'm not going to be able to help you." I stroked the golden hair out of his eyes and placed the stick in his mouth. "Close your eyes and think about something calm. I mean it. I need you to do this for me. Think about a warm beach with rolling waves or something."

"I'll try," he grunted around the stick in his mouth and closed his eyes.

Sending Cane to his happy place didn't really flood me with the calmness I needed, but it did seem to take the edge off of his fear.

"You too," I said to Aaron. "I need you feeling calm. Think about the beach. I mean *really* picture yourself there."

"Why?"

"Just do it, all right?" I snapped.

I took a couple of deep breaths to clear my head and then placed my hands over the leg again. The cold pain reached up for my fingers, and I felt around with my senses, letting them lap the edges of the pain until I could get a mental picture of the damage inside. When I had a good handle on what I was dealing with, I ramped up my concentration, drawing power from somewhere deep in my soul. My abdomen tightened and my own pain flared behind my eyes.

"Aaron, now!"

Aaron yanked on the leg and turned it straight. Cane

screamed in agony, dropping the stick. At the same time, I pushed with my determination and felt the heat tearing down my arms and out through my fingertips. I flooded the nerves with as much energy as I could to fight off the pain. Cool sweat beaded on my forehead from exertion as the tissue and bone wound its way back into place. My head spun dizzily, and I felt myself detaching from my body as if I were slipping into a dream. When I couldn't sustain the force anymore, I let go, sending the heat snapping back into me. This time, I collapsed.

# Chapter 25

THE PERSISTENT PAIN of a jack-hammer behind my eyes pulled me back to consciousness. In my bedroom, the soft light of morning filtered through my curtains bathing the bed in a rose-colored glow. I tried to stretch my tight muscles, but every part of my body ached.

I blinked to clear my vision, foggy from the migraine. Beside me, Monica dozed, dressed in a pair of my pajamas. Flashes of the night before came back to me, but all I could think about was my desperate need for anything to kill the pounding in my head. I was wearing a long t-shirt and no pants, and I wondered if Monica had gotten stuck changing me out of the bloody dress.

Tossing my covers back, I tried to sit up. The effort made me woozy, and I fell back down, waking Monica.

"You okay?" she asked, her voice dry from sleep.

"I have the world's worst headache." I moaned.

"I'll get you something for it. Where do you keep your Ibuprophen?"

I closed my eyes because the effort to hold them open was just too much. "Bathroom." I pointed in the vague direction.

Monica slipped off of the bed and disappeared. A moment later she returned with four tablets and a Dixie cup of water. I smiled in gratitude for the over-medication. She held my head so I could swallow.

"How are Bryan and Cane?" I asked as Monica crawled back under the covers on the opposite side of the bed.

"Bryan's sleeping in the guest room. He couldn't go back to his place all covered in blood and shirtless. Aaron said that your mom would never notice us here."

"And she didn't, did she?"

"No. She must have been sleeping when we got in. Anyway, Bryan carried you up here, and I did my best to clean up so you wouldn't wreck your sheets. Aaron gave him some clothes, and Bryan crashed out. He lost a lot of blood."

I cringed remembering the sticky puddle spread over the ground. It was amazing he was alive at all.

"It is really fixed, right?"

Monica nodded. "As far as we could tell. Aaron stayed with him for over an hour, but no bruise formed and Bryan said he felt fine."

The thought of almost losing him made my chest ache. At some point over these past few weeks, he had become something like a lifeline to me, the one bright spot in my otherwise dismal life. I needed him, sure, but I also felt the stirrings of what might be something more in my heart. I sighed. But if I liked Bryan, why had I kissed Cane?

As if reading my thoughts, Monica continued. "We took Cane home. He said if he went in by the patio door, he could get to his bedroom without his parents seeing him."

"So he can walk?" I asked.

"Yeah," she confirmed. "Good as new, I guess."

After a moment of silence, Monica asked in a timid voice, "Cady, what did you do last night? I mean, I watched it happen, but I don't know if I believe it yet."

"I don't know if I believe it either," I moaned, rolling onto my side.

I drifted off to sleep again without really answering her question.

I woke to find Bryan kneeling beside my bed, running his fingers along the side of my face. When my mouth curled into a grin, he stood and sat on the mattress next to my hip.

"Nice outfit." I commented.

He wore a pair of Aaron's sweatpants, too short by a few inches and one of my brother's zombie t-shirts. His hair stuck up in randomly spaced spikes that somehow worked on him. The warmth of his familiar presence flooded my soul, and I breathed deeply, as if I could suck more of it in.

"Thanks," he replied. "How are you feeling?"

My migraine was down from a ten to a three on the ouch-o-meter, but I was still weak. "A little better, I guess. I feel like I have a hangover without having had the fun of drinking."

He raised one of his brows, "Have you had a lot of hang-overs?"

I shook my head. "Once. The morning after our six-teenth birthday party. It wasn't pretty."

"Sounds like a good story."

"Maybe another day . . ." I rubbed the sleep out of the corners of my eyes.

Aaron came in carrying a tray of sandwiches. Monica followed with sodas. Bringing up the rear was Cane. A slight blush spread on his cheeks when his gaze met mine, and I knew we were both thinking about that kiss we shared. I bit my bottom lip to stop it from tingling with the memory. The warmth of Bryan's happiness burned me with guilt.

Bryan must have sensed something because he glanced back and forth between us with curiosity.

"Thought you could use some lunch," Monica said. "It'll help you get your energy back."

"I went in to see Mom a bit ago," Aaron explained, setting the tray on my bed and straddling my desk chair. "I told her we were out late after the dance, and Monica and Bryan decided to crash here. She didn't seem to care."

Cane cleared his throat. "I just stopped by to see how you're doing," he said without meeting my eyes.

He was too far away from me to get a reading, but he looked profoundly uncomfortable. Even after practically living at my house for half a year, I think it was the first time he'd ever been in my bedroom. Cane leaned against the back of my door as if afraid to come too far into the room. I saw his eyes flick to my hand wrapped in Bryan's.

Rising into a sitting position, I tucked the covers around my lower half. Monica sat down cross-legged on my bed like we were having a picnic or something. Cane waved away her offer to join us.

I picked up a peanut butter sandwich from the tray and bit into it eagerly, not realizing how hungry I was until the sweet grape jelly hit my tongue. Bryan popped open a soda can and handed it to me. The liquid tingled all the way down to my belly, making me feel more human already.

When we finished the sandwiches, Aaron set the tray on the floor and leveled his gaze on mine. "Okay, Cady. It's time that you tell us what happened last night."

I looked to Bryan for help, but his face was as expectant as everyone else's. How was I supposed to explain something that I didn't fully understand myself? I took a long swig of Diet Pepsi to buy some time.

"Well?" Aaron prodded, poking me in the foot.

I drew in a deep breath and let it out slowly. "I'm not a hundred percent sure, but I have a theory."

"Let's hear it."

I began to pick at my comforter to avoid looking at any of them. *It's like a Band-Aid, Cady. The quicker you tell them, the easier it'll be.*

"It started the night of Lony's accident," I explained.

Cane stiffened and his expression turned stoic. Neither of us wanted to remember that night, so I pushed on, telling them everything; the vision that sent me into the coma, the sensing of people's emotions, Jinx's explanation about my strange empathy . . . I even told them about Lucy and her tumor. Bryan nodded like a light had been turned on recalling that I'd mentioned Lucy to him before.

"So, I think somehow when I felt your pain, I was able to not only block it from myself, but to push it back entirely. And the energy that I felt flowing out of me and into Bryan and Cane, it was like I was giving them a piece of me . . . my life force or spirit or something. I know it sounds corny, but it's the best I can come up with."

When nobody said anything, I took the emotional temperature of the room. Bryan, Monica and Aaron all had a mixture of awe and skepticism to varying degrees. I still couldn't reach Cane, and his hard expression was unreadable. I grew more nervous in the silence. *That's it! They all think I'm crazy or lying or . . . both!*

Finally, Monica said with a little laugh, "Cady. You

want us to believe you're some sort of a psychic doctor or something?" She snorted in disbelief, but I could sense from the nervousness pooling in her direction that she believed me and that belief made her profoundly uncomfortable. She glanced at the guys to judge their reactions. Seeing something akin to acceptance on their faces, she continued, "Come on! I mean, how is it even possible?"

Surprisingly, Cane came to my defense first. "If I hadn't seen it with my own eyes —and felt the healing first-hand —I would've thought it was crazy too, but . . ." he paused. "I believe you, Cady. I have to."

"Same goes for me," Bryan agreed, patting my arm and grinning. "What you did last night? That was freaky, but I wouldn't be here right now if you hadn't saved me." He tipped my chin up with his finger and met my eyes. "Thank you, Cady."

For a moment, I basked in the rosy glow of his appreciation.

Aaron shook his head in disbelief. He tapped his fingers nervously on the back of his chair.

"I remember when you and Lon were little. You were so . . . I don't know . . . connected? Before you learned to talk for real, you had your own language that only the two of you could understand. I don't think you fully gave it up until you went to kindergarten. I used to get so mad that you wouldn't let me in on your secrets. The way you would just instinctively know what the other was feeling all of the time made me think I was stupid or something."

I opened my mouth to protest, but he held his hand up to stop me.

"What I'm saying is I knew you and Lony had this connection your whole lives. I guess I can see how your auras or minds or whatever would have reached out for each other at the time of her death. That had to have left a lasting effect on you. And since I don't have a better explanation for what happened last night, I have to believe you too, Sis."

Monica looked a little bit defeated but didn't say anything else.

"I'm exhausted, but I should probably get up." I said, stretching my arms out in front of me to loosen up my shoulders.

Aaron nodded. "I want to talk more about this, but I'll let you rest up for now. Oh, and Dad called a bit ago. He's coming over in a little while to talk to us about something." He patted my foot, placed the chair back under the desk and walked out, giving Cane a playful shuck to the bicep as he passed.

"I'm going to go change," Monica announced. She hopped off the bed and picked up her wrinkled party dress from the floor. She gave it a sniff and shrugged. "Bryan, I have to be to the airport by three. We should go soon."

"Okay," he replied and she slipped out the door.

Cane's mouth hardened into a line and he stepped toward me. As soon as he stepped into my range, my mouth dropped open in shock. His eyes burned with an inner heat that I'd never seen in him before. That heat rolled up and down my bare arms.

Noticing my reaction, Bryan's eyes darkened and his grip on my hand tightened. Cane either didn't notice or didn't care, because he continued to move closer, his hot gaze burning into mine. My heart was speeding, and my body suddenly felt feverish. Bryan rose to a standing position. His suddenly protective stance looked ridiculous in the too-short jogging pants.

"Can we talk?" Cane asked softly, his eyes never straying from mine. "Alone?"

The skin along my forearm and neck prickled as I felt Bryan's hackles rise. He didn't need to be an empath to feel the intensity of Cane's emotions, so plainly written as they were on his face. A cool tendril of jealousy wrapped itself around my waist and snaked up my spine.

I needed a moment of distance from both of them. "Can I have a minute to get dressed?" My voice came out breathless, and I hoped the boys didn't notice.

Cane dipped his head in a brief nod. "I'll just be in the hall."

Bryan didn't move; he just stood watching Cane leave the room. Without Cane's heat, my body shivered under Bryan's possessiveness. Honestly, it made me a little frustrated with him.

"You too," I said. "Out."

"Oh. Of course." He smiled as some of the light returned to his eyes. He placed a quick kiss on my head and headed for the door. He stopped before the door and turned to look at me. "If you don't want to talk to him alone, I can stay with you."

I rolled my eyes and sighed. "I've known Cane forever. Stop acting all jealous."

His brows shot up in a combination of surprise and amusement. "Me? Jealous?"

Laughing, I tossed my pillow at him. "Get out!"

He caught the pillow, hugged it to his chest and shut the door behind him as he left.

As drained as I was, I couldn't tamp down the itchy energy in my limbs. There were things that I needed to work out —starting with my new ability to heal people. And as much as I dreaded it, I knew Cane wanted to talk about that kiss. The warmth in my cheeks at the memory came from deep within me, causing my pulse to gallop. *Where are these feelings coming from?*

I whipped my covers back and got out of bed, holding onto my headboard until the room stopped spinning. When I was ready, I crossed to the dresser and began yanking out clothes. My skin beneath the t-shirt was tinged brownish-red and I knew I'd have to shower before going anywhere. I'd slept in my bra and the elastic bit into my skin in angry red welts. Replacing it with a cotton sports bra, I put the t-shirt I'd slept in back on for the time being and pulled on a well-worn pair of jeans. I glanced at myself in the mirror. The pretty curls from the night before were matted and stuck out at random odd angles. I ran a brush through as well as I could before steeling myself to face Cane.

I assumed he wanted to apologize for his behavior the night before, but judging from the scorching vibes he had been throwing off, it would probably be a lie. He didn't regret that kiss, and truth be told, neither did I. *What is wrong with me? I like Bryan Sullivan, not Cane Matthews!*

I closed my eyes and took ten deep yoga breaths in an attempt to clear my head. It didn't work.

"Cane," I called, knowing he was close by. "You can come in now."

With my hands folded behind my back, I leaned against my dresser for support. A few seconds later, the door knob turned. Cane stepped inside and shut it behind him again. With tentative steps, he approached me as if I were a wild animal about to bolt. My heart raced under his forceful stare and the hair on my arms stood on end.

"Since you can feel what I'm feeling, I guess there's

no point in hiding it," he said softly. "Don't worry, I know where things stand with you and Bryan. He's a decent guy. Not good enough for you, but . . ." He shrugged and gave a sad grin.

"Cane —"

He stood in front of me now, so close I could smell the woodsy scent of his soap. He placed the tip of his index finger to my mouth. "Wait. I have something I want to ask you. Do you remember the first time we met?"

Honestly, I didn't. I know we hadn't gone to the same junior high school, so it must have been sometime in ninth grade. I shook my head.

The ghost of a smile touched his lips. "I didn't think so. I'll have to tell you about it sometime when your boyfriend isn't pacing outside the door."

The thought of Bryan should have put a damper on the swell of heat rising in my chest, but it didn't. With Cane this close and his feelings for me so clear, I could do nothing but succumb to my echoing response. I clenched my hands together tighter to keep from reaching for him, from wrapping my arms around his broad shoulders, twining my fingers through his honey-colored hair and pulling him to me. My lips parted to speak, but no words would come.

Cane leaned in closer and spoke in a whisper. "I'm not sorry I kissed you, Cady. I want to be. I mean, I wish I hadn't been drunk, and I wish you had been a more willing participant —"

"You didn't think I was willing?"

He sucked in a quick breath and looked at me with eyes blazing green and gold. The hope he felt at my question was like ice water on my growing passion. I was with Bryan. I couldn't let Cane hope for more. It was never going to happen. I slipped out from where he had me cornered and put several feet of separation between us.

"I-I just mean," I stammered, eyes trained on the carpet between us. "It wasn't all your fault. I seem to recall taking my time in pushing you away."

Neither of us said anything for a minute. I didn't need to see his face to feel the weight of his eyes pinning me where I stood. I couldn't look at him. I feared if I did, I would launch myself into his arms. *Where in the hell are these feelings coming from?* Finally, he cleared his throat.

"I better go." The twinge of reluctance in his statement was palpable. "You should get some rest today."

He took a step toward me, but when I flinched, he stopped. A spark of something flashed in him and I immediately understood —he thought I was afraid of him.

"If you need anything, I'm only a phone call away."

With that he crossed the room and drew the door closed behind him.

I flopped down on my bed, drawing the spare pillow to my chest and pulled the covers up to my neck. My mind spun in a million different directions. *Please let me be wrong,* I silently pleaded. *I couldn't have read him right.* I rolled over and curled my knees up to my chest. Even worse was my response. I could barely admit it to myself, but there was no denying it. The feelings that swelled up inside me the night before when Cane pressed his lips to mine were the same ones that I felt when Bryan kissed me and held me close. Did I really have feelings for both of them, or was I reacting to something inside them? *Is any of it real? Did Cane really care about me or was he confusing his former feelings for my sister? Ugh!*

What was the good in knowing peoples' emotions if

I couldn't determine the thoughts and motivations driving them?

Remembering Bryan was still here, I got out of bed and made for the door. He stood with Monica and Aaron at the bottom of the steps in the foyer. He still had on my brother's t-shirt, but he'd put back on his pants from the night before. When he saw me, he came up the stairs and wrapped me into a big hug. I tipped my head back to look at him. His eyes were so dark the pupils blended with the irises, but they shone so brightly, I could see my guilty reflection staring back at me.

"I have to take Monica home so she can gather her things. Are you all right?"

Beneath that calm, Bryan-feeling, I could sense a bit of that lingering jealousy and a bit of embarrassment over allowing me to notice it. The warmth winding its way around me was him concentrating on his affection for me. He knew I was aware of his emotions, yet he tried to hide them from me anyway. I wasn't sure how I felt about that.

"I'm fine," I replied. "Just tired."

I plastered on a smile that I hoped did not appear fake.

"Okay," he said, giving me a quick peck on the lips. "I'll call you tonight."

"Bye, and have a good flight," I called as he and Monica left out the front door.

My headache was mostly gone now, but every muscle in my body hummed with fatigue. As much as I wanted to hang around the house brooding about my love life all day, there was a much more important matter to attend to. *Holy crap! I can heal people???*

I took as quick of a shower as my exhaustion would allow. Not bothering to dry my hair, I descended the stairs, heading for the front door.

"Hey, Bug," my dad's voice called from the living room. "Don't go anywhere yet. We need to talk to you."

I entered the room to see my parents sitting beside each other on the couch clutching hands, not in a romantic way, more like Mom was clinging to him for strength. She was dressed in jeans and a sweater and her hair was brushed. If it weren't for her too pale skin and lack of makeup, she would've appeared almost normal again.

Aaron sat in the recliner, his knee bouncing nervously. While not as volatile as most of my class rooms were, the emotions feeding into me were varied and jumbled. My belly knotted up with Mom's fear and embarrassment. My chest ached with Dad's concern and love for his family. And my shoulders tensed with Aaron's uncertainty. The combination made me want to hurl. Instead, I sat on the arm of my brother's chair, aligning myself with him.

"What is it?" I asked.

My parents exchanged a look before my mother's gaze became engrossed with her shoes.

"You both know that your mother hasn't been herself lately," Dad said, rubbing Mom's arm supportively. "I know you've been worried about her." He heaved a sigh before continuing. "We've talked it over and your mother has agreed to get help."

"I thought she already was seeing a therapist," Aaron said.

"She is, but we think she needs more help than an outpatient program can offer her."

Mom didn't seem to notice that they were discussing her as if she weren't in the room.

"What are you saying?" I asked. "That she needs in-patient treatment?"

"I-I'm going to check myself into a rehab facility today," Mom answered. My gasp had more to do with how difficult it was for her to admit that than any real surprise on my part.

"We've found a place in Minnesota that can offer her support for her substance abuse problems as well as grief counseling. I'm driving her up there today."

"How long are you going to be gone?" Aaron asked, leaning forward with his elbows on his knees.

"For as long as it takes," Mom whispered, gazing beyond us out the window.

"I'll be moving back home temporarily while your mother's gone to keep an eye on you both. I know you kids have had a lot to deal with on your own for these last weeks, but it's time that we pull together as a family and get through this."

I struggled to block out the swirl of emotions in the room so I could assess my own thoughts. Part of me was glad that my mom was getting help. I knew it was the right thing. But another part of me boiled with frustration that Aaron and I were expected to find our way back to normal life on our own, while she was allowed to completely flake out. We didn't have the luxury of self-pity; we had school. And what about the crap I'd been living through these last weeks? My parents had no idea about the emotional rollercoaster I'd been on. Okay, so I hadn't exactly told them about it, but they hadn't thought to ask either.

I looked down at my brother sitting next to me, and the wind went out of my sails. Soft gray smudges spread under his eyes, dimming his inner light. I opened myself to him and felt the sadness and worry lingering in him as if it had taken up permanent residence. *I'm as bad as they are,* I thought. *So wrapped up in my own problems, I haven't been there for Aaron.* I rested my palm on his shoulder and silently vowed to be a better sister.

"I'm glad that you're getting help, Mom," he assured her. "Don't worry about us. Cady and I have each other's backs."

Dad nodded as if that settled everything. "Well, Julia, let's get your bags in the car and head out. It's over three hours to Rochester."

Mom stood and crossed to hug us, but I shirked away and went back up to my bedroom. I sat on the bed trying to understand why I was so angry with her, why I couldn't let myself feel sorry for her. *Guess sympathy doesn't automatically come with empathy.*

I lay back on my bed and covered my eyes with my forearm. The sounds of my parents gathering Mom's luggage from the bedroom down the hall echoed through the plaster walls. Just as I thought they had gone back down the stairs, a soft knock rapped on my door.

"Can I come in?" Mom asked, stepping inside without waiting for permission.

"Can I say no?" I sat up, my head dizzy from the movement. Man, I was exhausted. Not sleepy, just spent. I tried to block out her feelings, but I couldn't do it anymore. Her guilt and pain and sorrow seeped around my shields, demanding my attention. The emotions weakened me further, so I dropped the blocks, letting them flood over my mind in defeat.

"Cady, I know you are worried about me —"

"I'm not worried, I'm pissed off. Big difference."

Mom sat down on the bed next to me and tried to put

her arm around my shoulders, but I shot to my feet, putting distance between us. I couldn't let her touch me. I had enough of an emotional storm brewing on my own; I didn't want direct contact with her to drag me into her pity-party, invalidating my own feelings.

"Arcadia—"

"Will you please stop that? Stop using that mother-voice on me. It's not going to work, all right?" I paced back and forth in front of my closet.

"I am your mother," she said, her voice rising with indignation.

I paused mid-stride and faced her. "Really? Some mother you've been lately. Tell me, while you were wallowing away in your bedroom like some Victorian-era heroine, did you even think about the two kids that you left to fend for themselves?"

I hated myself even as I was doing it, but something snapped within me, and I let it all out. "Who do you think paid the bills this month? Dad did. Who has been making excuses for you when your office calls, or the clients that you have abandoned? Aaron, that's who. Who has been making sure there is food in the house? Me."

The volume of my voice was steadily rising into a shout. "We're all running around here taking care of things so you don't have to. So you can feel sorry for yourself. But what about us? We lost someone too. You do not have a monopoly on loving her!"

Mom's skin faded to a grayish white and her hands visibly shook. I had gone too far. I'd kicked her when she was down. What kind of shitty daughter does that?

Dad appeared at the door. The tight press of his lips let me know he'd heard at least part of my tirade. "You ready to head out, Julia?"

Mom stood, smoothing her clothes, not meeting either of our eyes. She nodded.

"Mom," I said, reaching for her as she brushed past me. She yanked her arm from my grasp, leveled her lightly blood shot eyes on me and said, "Goodbye, Arcadia."

The odd formality in her tone rooted me to the spot, keeping me from following them out the door, down the steps and to the car.

I crossed the hall to the guest bedroom and watched from the window. In the driveway, Aaron hugged Mom tightly and Dad tucked her into the passenger seat of his truck as if she were fragile cargo. Aaron waved until the truck turned out of sight.

I slumped down to the floor, drawing my knees to my chest, too upset to even cry. I never had temper problems before, but for the second time since the accident, I found myself feeling guilty and embarrassed by a sudden outburst. It wasn't like me at all.

A long sigh from the doorway made me look up.

"So now what?" Aaron asked.

"Huh?"

He entered the room and sat down on the carpet near me. "Well, one of my sisters is gone, and I can't do anything about it. My mother has a drug problem and is headed to re-hab, and I can't do anything about it. My other sister," he cut his eyes to me, "has turned into some sort of psychic healer, and I probably can't do anything about that either, but well, I'm here and so are you, so I guess that means we're in this together. So again, what do we do now?"

"Now," I shrugged. "It's time to figure out what in the

hell happened last night."

Aaron's head nodded in agreement. "Okay. Where do we start?"

I grinned. "I think it's time for you to meet the neighbor."

# Acknowledgements

IF IT TAKES a village to raise a child, it takes at least an apartment building filled with an eclectic bunch of neighbors to publish a book. I give my appreciation and thanks to the following people who played a part in *Arcadia's Gift*.

First and foremost, I'd like to thank my writing group Mercy Loomis, R. Scott Steele and Joe "Zombie Joe" Alfano. They saw the most horrendous versions of this story and still chose to support me. Thank you for your input and peer pressure. Sometimes, not wanting to show up empty-handed on Tuesday night was all that kept me going. A special thanks to you, ZJ, for helping me out of my title crisis and for your phenomenal baking. Seriously, your cupcakes are like ambrosia.

Thank you to my editor, Vicki Keire. Your comments, suggestions and support were valuable to me. I look forward to working with you again in the future.

Even with a fabulous editor, it is essential to gather input from others. Thank you to all of those who beta read for me: Victoria Grundle, Elyse Rector, Mercy Loomis, Jennifer Lowe, Tammy Treleven and Ashlyn Rae —who helped me with getting the teen perspective right.

Thank you to Phatpuppy Art for my gorgeous cover. Every time I look at it I feel like Cady is alive and not just a fictional character born of my imagination.

On a personal level, I need to thank my longsuffering husband, Steve Riggles. You never complain about the time I spend in front of my laptop or running around with my bookish friends. I couldn't wish for a more supportive man in my life.

Speaking of bookish friends . . . thank you to Victoria Grundle, Lindsey Hebel, Jamie Annear-Feyrer, Laura Kate Leibelt and Mercy Loomis for our book club. That one night each month has kept me sane through this whole process. I love you all like sisters!

Lastly, I want to thank Eleah, Eliesha and Michael Dickenson for educating me on what it means to be a twin and how powerful the connection between twins can be. I don't think those of us who are not a twin can fully understand the relationship. I hope this story in some small way honors that special bond.

Okay, enough of the love fest. I have another book to write.


~Jesi Lea Ryan

# Arcadia's Gift
# Playlist

Music is powerful inspiration for writers. The following are the songs that provided fuel for my imagination during the writing of *Arcadia's Gift*. They are also the music most likely to be on Cady's iPod. (In no particular order.)

*Teenage Love* - Lee MacDougall
*Hurricane Drunk* - Florence + the Machine
*If I Die Young* - The Band Perry
*Handlebars* - Flobots
*Run* - Snow Patrol
*Mad World* - Gary Jules
*I Lay My Head* - Fallulah
*Return* - Ok Go
*Bizarre Love Triangle* - New Order
*Calling You* - Blue October
*End of the Dream* - Evanescence
*Shadow of the Day* - Linkin Park
*How* - Regina Spektor
*Trumpet Vine* - A Stick and A Stone
*Kiss Me* - Ed Sheeran
*Sleep* - The Dandy Warhols

# About the Author

JESI LEA RYAN grew up in the Mississippi River town of Dubuque, IA. She holds bachelor degrees in creative writing and literature and a masters degree in business. She considers herself a well-rounded nerd who can spend hours on the internet researching things like British history, anthropology of ancient people, geography of random parts of the world, bad tattoos and the paranormal. She currently lives in Madison, WI with her husband and two exceptionally naughty kitties.

### Stalk Jesi online at . . .
www.jesilea.com
Twitter @Jesilea
Facebook: https://www.facebook.com/pages/Jesi-Lea-Ryan/152086598147945
Tumblr

### More from Jesi . . .
*Arcadia's Curse: Arcadia - Book 2*
*Arcadia's Choice: Arcadia - Book 3*

And don't miss the FREE short prequel story . . . .
*The End of the Line: Arcadia - Book 0.5*